PROSPECT

KINGS OF RETRIBUTION MC MONTANA

CRYSTAL DANIELS

SANDY ALVAREZ

TWO PENS-

CRYSTAL Daniels

Sandy ALVAREZ

-ONE STORY

1

SAM

If anyone had told me a few years ago I'd be where I am today, I would have laughed in their face. That's the funny thing about life though; it never goes according to plan. I learned a long damn time ago to stop trying to map out my future, because the moment you think you have it all figured out, you're thrown a curveball. That curveball usually leaves behind a trail of destruction more times than not.

Something else I learned is there is always a reward waiting for you on the flip side of said destruction. We have to walk through hell on earth now and then to claim the reward our maker has destined for us. My reward? The Kings of Retribution MC. The club is more like a family to me than the one I share blood with. The Kings have become my home. I left Texas the moment I graduated high school. For as long as I can remember, I knew I didn't want the same things in life as my father. I also knew he didn't give a damn about what I wanted and had been planning my future since the day I was born.

One thing my father didn't count on was his only son had no desire to be his puppet. I busted my ass in high school playing football; a sport I didn't particularly like but discovered pretty quickly was good at. I used my skills to award me a full-ride scholarship to three different colleges of my choosing. Picking the school furthest away from home, I chose Montana State University. To say my dad flipped his shit would be an understatement. My father took little interest in my football career and had no idea how good I was. He always assumed I would do what was expected of me and attend his alma mater Texas State University. Once he learned of my scholarship and that I no longer needed him or his money, he sang a whole different tune. My dad played off my going against his will as me needing to sow my wild oats before coming back to Texas, and taking my place in the family business alongside him. I walked out of the house I had grown up in, climbed into the truck my mother had bought for me a year before she passed away and made the two-day drive to Bozeman Montana. I haven't looked back since.

Looking back now, I can't believe I made it through my last year of high school and my first year of college. The way I allowed my life to spiral out of control the two years following my mother's death fills me with regret. It was the summer before my second year at Bozeman University that things changed for me. My drinking had gotten out of control. I was showing up to my classes and football practice every day hungover. Hell, sometimes, I was still drunk. I was on thin ice with my coach, and my professors had long given up on me. I didn't care though. I wanted to forget. I tried to drown out the pain of losing my mom. My mother was the most important person in my life. She was a constant—the one person I could always depend on. The truth was, I didn't know how to cope with her being gone, and forgetting seemed like my best bet at the time. The tipping point of my downward spiral was the night I decided to mix my booze with coke. The entire night was a blur. I woke up the next morning naked in a stranger's bed, two strangers to be exact; some guy and his girlfriend.

I knew then that my drinking had gone too far. Sure, I had bedded more girls than I can count; girls I never bothered to remember the names of. But waking up with another guy? Let's just say that was a massive eye-opener for me. The guy and his girl assured me that yes, we had shared his girlfriend, but nothing happened between him and me, and I believed them. It's not just the waking up naked next to a man, but the fact that I was engaging in sex without having any memory of it and not knowing whether or not I was using protection. The first thing I did after sobering up was I got myself checked at the clinic. The following week while waiting on my test results was the longest week of my entire life. Luckily my tests came back clean. From that moment on, the heavy drinking and the random sex stopped. I had to take back control of my life.

It was when the new semester of school had started I met Alba. I don't know what led me to walk up to her and strike up a conversation that day in class. All I knew was that there was this shy girl who looked like she was somewhere she didn't belong, kind of like me. So, I guess that's why I was drawn to her. But not in a way that said I was attracted to her, but in a way that said she was just the kind of friend I needed. I could tell by the very first moment she looked at me she wasn't like the rest of the girls at school; the kind of girl that sniffed around us athletes looking to score. No, this girl needed a friend, same as me. And that's what we became—friends. Although, I would say Alba is more like a sister. I believe it was fate that led us to become friends. It is because of her that I am where I'm at today.

Circumstances in Alba's life led her to leave college and return home to Polson. Not long after she left Bozeman, I quit school and followed her. Like my best friend, school wasn't for me. Alba introduced me to her family, who happens to be bikers. She is now married to one of them, Gabriel Martinez. Gabriel is the Enforcer for The Kings of Retribution MC. Then you have The Kings

President, Jake, their Vice President, Logan, Srg. At Arms, Quinn, and their Road Captain, Reid. You also have Bennett and his wife, Lisa. Bella is Alba's sister, and she is married to Logan. Reid is married to Mila, Quinn is married to Emerson and Jake is married to Grace. A few of the other guys like Blake, Grey, and Austin are still single. Toss in all their rugrats, and you have the entire King family. Then you have the single most important member of The King family. The girl who has become my obsession.

Sofia Torres.

My Firefly.

The first time I laid eyes on Sofia was a few weeks after I moved to Polson. Bella, Alba's sister, was having a family dinner at her and Logan's house. The sun had just set, and everyone was milling around the backyard tossing back beers and engaging in conversation. I was sitting on the deck next to Alba when a lone figure standing alone by the edge of the lake caught my attention. The girl with her back to me stood at 5 feet 2 inches and had long dark hair that hung almost to her waist. There was something about this girl that called to me. On autopilot, I stood from my seat and strode across the yard in her direction. I faintly remember hearing Alba tell me her name was Sofia. At that moment, all the noise around me ceased to exist. The only sound that could be heard was the beating of my own heart. It was when I was about ten feet from Sofia when I stopped and stared at her.

With her back still facing me, all I could see was her profile. I watched as she looked with wonderment at the fireflies dancing over the lake. A minute later, when she felt my presence and looked over at me with the brightest smile, I felt as though I had been punched in the stomach. It wasn't just Sofia's beauty that had rendered me speechless; it was the way she lit up at something as simple as watching fireflies.

Letting off the throttle, I pull up to Grace's bakery, park, and climb off my bike. What can I say, the club has worn off on me. I bought my Harley last year, and my bike has become an extension of me. In high school, I had a Kawasaki Ninja 300. My friends and I used to race them on the weekends. It was more of a hobby back then. I haven't ridden a bike in years, but being around the guys made me realize how much I missed it. The guys at Kings Custom had bought the bike when it was a piece of shit scrap of metal. They like to find old treasures, fix them up and sell them. When the bike was finished, I knew the moment I saw it that I wanted it to be mine. Jake and the rest of the men didn't rib on me when I came to them about it. I figured they would since I knew how most of the people around town saw me. I was a college kid, the guy who was best friends with one of their old ladies. But to my surprise, Jake clapped me on my back and said, "You got it, son."

It was then I realized the guys hadn't made any assumptions about me. I wish I could say the same for my best friend. Not that I'm mad. It's pretty fucking funny. It was Jake who came to me one day at a family party and told me Alba and our friend Leah had told the guys I was gay. I nearly choked on my damn beer when those words spilled from his mouth. But the President of The Kings of Retribution wasn't there to confirm my sexual preference; he was there to threaten my balls if I hurt Sofia. It seems my interest in my Firefly hadn't gone unnoticed. I told Jake and the rest of the men they had nothing to worry about. I'd die before I ever allowed anything or anyone to hurt Sofia.

Striding into the bakery, the bell over the door alerts Grace to my arrival. "Good morning, Sam."

"Mornin', Grace."

"The usual?" she questions.

"Yes, ma'am." Grace gives me a warm smile as she places two chocolate croissants into a small bag and hands it over. Once I've paid for my purchase, I tip my head. "I'll see you tomorrow."

"Bye, Sam."

Climbing on my bike, I start her up and make my way toward

New Hope House. Sofia has been doing amazing things with the foundation. So much so she is having additional rooms built on to the place. Kings Construction is in charge of the project. I was hired at Kings Construction when I moved to Polson. I worked for a contractor in Bozeman for a few months after I dropped out of school. Being impressed with my work since I started, Reid decided to put me in charge of the job at New Hope House.

As always, I'm the first to arrive at Sofia's. Just as I'm making my way around to the back of the house, my cell rings. Pulling it from my pocket, I answer. "Yeah?"

"I need you down at the office," is Reid's curt reply.

"On my way."

Hanging up the phone, I continue up the steps to the back porch and place the bag with the chocolate croissants on the railing.

Fifteen minutes later, I'm strolling into Kings Construction when my friend and roommate Leah greets me.

"Reid is waiting for you in his office," she says in a low tone. Alba and I met Leah at the University. She is the main reason I moved to Polson. Long story short, Leah is hiding from her father. Leah's story is hers to tell, but she lives here in Polson under the protection of the club and myself.

I knock on Reid's office door. "You wanted to see me?"

"Yeah, come on in," he nods, and I sit on the chair across from his desk.

"We signed off on a new contract yesterday. You remember the guy whose resort we did some work on?" Reid asks, and I nod. "Well, he's decided he wants a house built. It turns out he bought some land out by the lake and wants us to head up the project."

"That's great. What do you need from me?"

"I know you're busy down at New Hope House, but I want you to go out to the site with Nikolai and meet up with the architect. You have proven yourself to be a vital part of this company, and I'd like to bring you in on other aspects of the job. I want you to head up this next project with Nikolai. The construction won't start for another few months, so you will have time to finish up at Sofia's. In the meantime, I want you sitting in on all the happenings with the O'Connell project," Reid finishes.

Masking my shocked expression, I stand and offer Reid my hand. "Thank you for this opportunity. I won't let you down."

When I walk out of Reid's office and to the front, I find a very intense looking Nikolai. Only his attention is not on me. At the moment, Nikolai's entire focus is on my friend. Standing in front of her desk, he doesn't bother with hiding the fact he's staring at Leah, who is looking uncomfortable. I can't help but chuckle because her face is beet red and she refuses to take her eyes off her lap. "You with me today?" Nikolai asks, finally acknowledging my presence.

"Yeah. You ready?" Nodding, Nikolai turns walking out the door, and I follow behind.

It's nearly 6:00 pm when I roll up to the clubhouse. The guys stop by here after work for a beer or two before going home to their women. I haven't missed one night since I was invited into their fold about six months ago. I climb off my bike the same moment Lisa steps outside.

"Hi, Sam." She smiles. I learned a long time ago, Lisa is the momma bear of the club. Her motherly smile reminds me a lot of my mom.

"Ma'am." I smile in return, tipping my head.

"How many times have I told you, young man, to call me Lisa?"

"More times than I can count, Mrs. Lisa, but my mom raised me right. Plus, those old southern habits are hard to break."

"I suppose you're right. Manners can be hard to come by these days."

"Yes, ma'am, they are." I grin, and Lisa pats my arm. "Don't change for anyone, Sam."

"I won't. You have a good night, Mrs. Lisa."

"You too, honey."

Walking into the clubhouse, Jake is the first to greet me. He tips his chin. "Son."

"Sir," I speak and offer my hand the same way I do every time I'm in his presence. "Have a seat, " he says, clapping my back and gesturing to the stool beside him. Ember, one of the club girls, hands me a beer. I tip my bottle, acknowledging Logan, Gabriel, Reid, Blake, Austin, and Bennett, who are all seated at the bar. After taking a swig of my beer, I turn to Gabriel. "How's Alba? I haven't called her in a couple of days."

"She's good," he grunts. "She said she was going to call you for a visit and invite you to supper this week. Just a heads up on that."

A second later, the clubhouse door swings open and in walks Quinn. "Hey, you assholes didn't talk to him without me, did ya?" he says with a big-ass grin.

"You got here just in time," Jake replies. "I was just about to ask him."

I look around at the guys to find them eyeing me. "What's going on?" One by one, the men stand from their stools and form a line in front of me. I also notice Ember making a quiet retreat out of the room.

Jake is the first to speak. "I had a meetin' with my brothers the other day. You see, over the past year or so, I have watched you become an important member of this family. You have proven time and time again that you care about the people in this club and our community. I knew the first time you showed up at my clubhouse riskin' your ass for your friend and Gabriel's old lady, that you're a solid guy. With that said, me and my men have come to the same assessment."

I cut my eyes down the line, glancing at each of the guys, who are all wearing their best poker face. All except Quinn, who is still sporting a big ass grin. "What assessment?" I ask with what I'm sure is a confused look on my face.

"That you are just what this club needs, and we'd like you to be one of us. We want you to prospect for The Kings," Jake answers in a no bullshit tone that says he is not joking. "We'll give you twenty-four hours to give us your answer."

"I don't need twenty-four hours. My answer is yes." I don't try to hide my smile or the pride I'm feeling. The club is coming to me and offering the opportunity to become one of them. My answer is a no brainer. The room erupts into a round of cheers.

"You show us you have what it takes to be a prospect and that you are willin' to put this club above all else, and we'd be damn proud to call you brother one day."

"I'm ready to prove myself, Jake. You can count on me," I declare.

"I know you are, son. Just know there will be no special treatment. You will be treated like any other prospect. You will pay your dues just as the rest of the brothers have. I don't care if one of my men asks you to polish his bike with your dick swingin' in the breeze. You'll do so without belly-achin' and a smile on your face. You got me?" Jake squares off.

"Yes, sir. I got you."

"Good. Now go home and pack your shit. I want you moved into the clubhouse by Saturday."

2

SOFIA

S tretching, I roll onto my back. The warm glow of the sunrise is just beginning to peek through the sheer yellow curtains in my bedroom. I lay there snuggled amongst the softness of my white down comforter and listen to the soft whirring sound of the oscillating fan and watch my room come alive with a prism of colors dancing across my pale grey walls from the firefly sun-catcher hanging in front of the window. Closing my eyes, I take in a deep, cleansing breath. I always try to begin my day with gratitude, thankful for another day of a life I fought so hard to stay alive for.

Slipping from beneath the comforter, I swing my legs over the edge of the bed, curling my toes into the soft shag carpet beneath my feet as I stand. Before anything else, I spin around and begin making my bed. When I've fluffed the last pillow and flawlessly place it on the bed, I slip on my house slippers and shuffle toward the door unlocking it. I know I'm safe, but locking my bedroom door gives me an added sense of security.

Leaving the door open, I walk down the hallway. After making a quick stop by the bathroom to wash my face, brush my teeth, and take care of other business, I continue my way toward the kitchen. I have been living at New Hope House for a few months now. I've accomplished a lot in the time I have been living in Polson by graduating high school and slowly reaching milestones with my therapy, which is why Dr. Kendrick, my therapist suggested I take a significant step on my way to independence. I already spent so much of my time here anyway, so along with the support of my friends and family, I moved out of Logan and Bella's home and into New Hope House.

As scary as it was in the beginning, it was the small nudge I needed toward so many more future goals. Another plus to living here is seeing Dr. Kendrick daily. Not that I always need to talk with her, but it is good to know I can walk right down the hallway, across the living room and straight into her office.

Also, I've recently applied for online courses to become a counselor myself. I know it will take time and hard work, but I'm willing to do it. Helping others and giving back to the community that has helped me is what I want to do with my life. I've watched how The Kings and the staff at New Hope House changed lives in this small town, and I want to be a part of it.

Busying myself with what has become my morning routine, I start making coffee and go through the refrigerator and pantry taking stock of things we will need to pick up from the grocery store later today before I go into work. I have a part-time job at The Pier, which is a small family-owned restaurant on Polson Bay. I work there four days a week and I love it. It's usually always busy, but when the summer months hit, they stay packed. The best part of the job is the view. Open skies and open water. The sun and the fresh Montana air. There is nothing better. Sometimes, after my shift is over, I sit out at the end of the dock and watch the sun kiss the surface of the water and wait for the fireflies to come out.

Filling the tea kettle with water, I set it on the stovetop and light the fire beneath it. While most of the people in my life are coffee drinkers, I prefer a warm cup of chai tea sweetened with honey in the mornings. As I am searching for my favorite mug inside the dishwasher, I hear the unmistakable rumble of Sam's motorcycle pulling into the driveway. Kings Construction is adding a new addition to the house, and Sam happens to be heading up the job and given his own crew. Peeking out the window above the sink, I watch as he rounds the corner of the deck in the backyard. It's odd, the feelings I've developed for him. I'm not used to them. Not that I don't know what they are; trust me, I do. But to be honest, I never thought I would want to feel this way for a man. Sam makes me feel safe and comfortable in my own skin. He doesn't look at me like I'm damaged goods.

Sam is also a handsome guy. Tall, dark hair, chiseled chin, an athletic build, and he has blue eyes the color of sapphires. Keeping my eyes on him, I watch as he places a small white paper bag on the back deck railing. The corner of his lip lifts in a subdued smile as he does so. I hold my breath, thinking this time he has spotted me in the window, but he continues walking toward the building site on the other end of the house allowing me to breathe again. Wearing a smile on my face and feeling butterflies in my stomach, I walk over to the French doors near the kitchen table which lead out to the deck. Unlocking the deadbolt, I step out into the fresh morning air, pausing a moment as the warmth from the sun touches my skin. Knowing Sam is watching me, I cross the deck, past the patio chairs, stopping at the railing. Picking the white bag up, I open it and peer inside. The smell from the warm chocolate croissants instantly causes my mouth to water. These croissants have become my favorite guilty pleasure from Grace's bakery, The Cookie Jar, since coming to live in Polson. And every morning since Sam started construction on the house, he has brought me my favorite treat.

Turning, with my breakfast clutched in my hand, tucked close to my chest, I lift my head in Sam's direction, briefly making eye contact with him. It's moments like this, I feel a little awkward, shy, and unsure of myself. Giving him a small smile, I walk back inside, locking the door behind me.

The tea kettle whistles. Sitting the bag on the table, I walk across the kitchen and turn the burner off. Pouring the hot water into my mug, I carry my steaming cup of tea to the table. With the sounds of Sam's work crew arriving and their workday getting underway, I sip my drink then retrieve a pastry from the bag.

"Good morning, Sofia," Emma, a woman living here at New Hope softly says as she enters the kitchen. Reaching into the cabinet above the coffee maker, she grabs a mug pouring herself some coffee before joining me at the kitchen table.

"How are you feeling this morning?" I ask, knowing she has an interview later today here in town at the local library.

"Nervous." Her hands grip tightly around the cup as she brings the rim to her lips, taking a small sip.

"You have nothing to worry about," I assure her.

"Finally doing something for myself without the fear of always having to look over my shoulder is an entirely new concept for me to get used to," she confesses.

Emma suffered several years of abuse at the hands of her now ex-husband. The last beating she endured landed her in the hospital with severe injuries, which took her weeks to heal from. Now, with him finally behind bars and the help and support of the foundation, she is starting her life over.

Finished with my breakfast, I stand, throwing my trash into the garbage bin. "I want to hear all about your new job later today." I smile warmly in Emma's direction.

She laughs. "The job isn't mine yet."

"I have faith in you. You are perfect for the library assistant job, and I have no worries that you'll be hired on the spot."

"Your confidence means a lot, Sofia. Thank you," Emma gives me a small smile.

Taking my tea with me, I make my way back to my room. After changing out of my sleep shorts and oversized shirt, I slip on a lilac-colored, boho style summer dress and pair it with nude-colored strappy sandals. Standing in front of my full-length mirror, I brush my long hair before securing it into a low ponytail. Not one to wear a lot of makeup, I apply moisturizer, brush a light coat of mascara on my lashes and swipe a light tinted gloss across my top and bottom lip.

Satisfied, I open my door and walk across the hall to the empty room. A new resident is scheduled to arrive late this afternoon, so I need to prepare her room by putting linens on the bed. Walking to the closet, I dig out the new, unopened bed sheets along with a quilt Mila left that once belonged to her grandmother; the one this very foundation was named after. Getting to work, I pull the sheets from their packaging. Whipping the fitted sheet in the air unraveling it, I spread it across the full-sized mattress pulling the corners taught before moving on to the top sheet and finally the quilt.

Luna is the name of the young woman Dr. Kendrick will be bringing in today. I haven't been told much about her. Only that she is not from Polson, she's deaf, and she is in hiding from her ex-boyfriend, who is currently sitting in jail, and Luna is the only witness to the crime that landed him there. Luna didn't feel safe staying where she lived because of the connections her ex has. One of the detectives on her ex's case is an old friend of Dr. Kendrick. She is the one that suggested New Hope House. I'm reassured by The Kings' presence here in town and the top-notch security we have here at the house that this is a safe place for her.

My mind starts to wander back in time to my own life and the fear I lived in for two years. Without warning, unwanted memories from my past hit me like a tidal wave.

Slowly sinking to the bed, I struggle to gain control of the flashbacks that sometimes still plague me. Anxiety and panic can hit without warning, sending me into the state I'm in now. Closing my eyes, I take long breaths through my nose and release an even longer lung full of air out my mouth. I do this several times trying to slow the rapid beating in my chest. Trying to center myself is the hardest part of getting through a panic attack. With so many thoughts and emotions hitting me at once, it is always a struggle to remain focused on one thought that doesn't sound negative. Bring in the fact I usually freak out by the way my body physically reacts, and I sometimes quickly start thinking something else is wrong with me as well. That then creates a continuous loop, making it harder to break free from the crippling hold my anxiety and mind has on me. These vulnerable moments are flaws of mine that have become hard to accept, and I will probably live with it for the rest of my life. PTSD that is related to my childhood and my time with Los Demonios.

Los Demonios. The name of my demons who haunt me. They are the ones who, even now in their deaths, still control part of my life. They stole me from my family, from the only life I knew. Taking me as payment for what my father did. My life was never perfect. My family was poor, and I recognized the daily struggles my parents went through from an early age to keep a roof over our heads and food on the table. Los Demonios ran things in the town where my family lived in Mexico. They were feared and ruthless in the way they ran things. What my mother didn't know was my father had gone to them out of desperation one day, begging for a job. So, they gave him one. I'm still not sure to this day what it was he was doing for them, but I know it was not good. Nothing good came from being associated with Los Demonios.

One night, just after my fourteenth birthday, I was awakened by my father and mother and not allowed to ask why we left our home under the dark of night. It was when we had made our way to the border did I realize what we were about to do. Not everyone crosses the border undetected, but we were lucky. Without hesitation, we left behind our homeland, and I never asked why.

Almost a year later, after seeking asylum, which was still pending at the time, things were going okay. My father was working for a small landscape company, and my mother had found work at a restaurant waiting tables. As for me, my parents had enrolled me in school. We lived with another family, and my life, even though we didn't have much, was better than it ever was in Mexico.

Little did I know what my father had done—until the day faces of men I thought we had left behind showed up one evening as we were sitting down for dinner.

One face always stood out amongst the rest. I didn't know his name at the time, but back in Mexico, I noticed he was always around—always watching me. He was a member of Los Demonios.

They entered our home, forcing my mother and me to watch as they beat my father. The entire time the President sat back, demanding to know where his money was. It wasn't until my father's blood covered the tiled floor did he confess he took the money, and it was gone, shocking both my mother and me with his admission. My father committed a crime—he stole money from the notorious Los Demonios.

That night changed my life.

With a nod from his leader, I was snatched from my mother's embrace by the man who always watched me from afar, who I now know to be Antonio. I remember the struggle as I tried to go back to her.

Now you will pay with your life and the life of your daughter for what you have done.

My mother's wails still resonate as strong as the day it happened. Antonio stood there over my father, who was on his knees, pleading for my life over his own, but it was of no use.

Antonio forcefully lead me out of the house and into the cold night. A single gunshot sliced through the night air like a lightning strike.

I feel suspended in time as all these moments in my life collide in my mind. It's one of several flashbacks I continue to have.

A small voice keeps telling me to breathe. It is not until my heartbeat slows do I recognize it as my own.

Unless someone knows my story, they would never know all I have overcome and my journey through hell. I win tiny battles against them and myself every day. The way your mind adapts to coping and surviving also shrouds a lot of ugly to protect you and sometimes even tricks you into thinking you are always okay, when honestly, some days, I'm not. But I am determined to be, and that is what matters.

3

SAM

I wake first thing Saturday morning to my cell ringing. Reaching over, I grab it from the table beside my bed to see my father's name lighting the screen, and I immediately send it to voicemail. I have been avoiding his calls for months now. I know what he wants. He wants me to come home and, for whatever reason, has been more persistent lately. That leads me to believe there is something more behind his recent calls. A moment later, the phone rings again. This time I answer. "Dad." My voice is cold and detached.

"You know I'm tired of your games, Sam. When I call, you answer."

"I don't answer to you. I haven't for a long time," I say, cutting him off.

"Stop acting like a spoiled little shit. I don't have time for it."

"Then stop fuckin' calling me," I grind out.

"You have an obligation to this family, Sam. It's time you come home."

"I'm good where I'm at. I think I'll stay here."

"Goddamnit, Sam!" my father roars on the other end of the line. Not in the mood for his tirade, I hang up.

Tossing my phone on the bed beside me, I run my palm down my face and let out a heavy sigh. I know ignoring my father won't make him go away, but I have reached a point where I don't have the energy to give a damn. Pushing aside the nagging feeling in the pit of my stomach that my father will stir up shit, I stand and head to the bathroom for a shower. Stripping out of my briefs, I step into the stall and under the spray of hot water. The heat does little to ease the tension in my shoulders. Shaking thoughts of my dad away, I focus on my tasks for today. I will be moving into the clubhouse this morning and officially become a prospect for The Kings.

The club is where my loyalty lies. They are the ones who matter. Those men have treated me like family from day one. They have never asked for anything in return and have no hidden agenda. I wish I could say the same about my father. He doesn't give a shit about anyone but himself. He only pretends to care when he wants something. Just like he did with my mother, he used her up until there was nothing left but a shell of a woman. When she died, all my dad cared about was how her death affected his reputation. People back in Texas only saw a perfect family when it came to the McGregor's. They never saw the kind of man William McGregor was. I vow never to be anything like him.

Once I'm finished with my shower and dressed, I walk out of my room and make my way into the kitchen to find Leah sitting at the island drinking a cup of coffee. "Hey, darlin'."

"Morning." She smiles.

Pouring myself a cup, I then turn, face my friend and eye her over the rim of my cup. We talked about my moving out last night. Leah put on a brave face and assured me she was cool with living in our apartment on her own, but she is not good at masking her feelings. I know she's scared. "Will you stop looking at me like that," she fusses. "I'll be fine, Sam. Quit treating me like some fragile, broken girl who can't take care of herself."

"I don't think of you like that, Leah." Setting my cup down, I look her in the eyes. "You are one of the strongest people I know. But you're also my friend, and I will always look out for you. You're like a sister to me, Leah." Her face softens at my words.

"I know. You're like a brother to me, which is why I'm happy for you. I'm happy you're moving on. Now go on and finish packing. Stop worrying about me. I'll be fine."

I kiss the top of her head. "Okay. If at any time you need anything, you call. The clubhouse is only five minutes away. Understand?" I say, and she nods. I'll make a point to talk to Jake about the situation and find out what can be done to make sure Leah feels safe and comfortable about living on her own.

An hour later, I stroll into the clubhouse with my bags in tow. The moment I step inside, I'm welcomed by the guys pounding their fists on the bar while Jake steps forward with a cut fisted in his hand. Dropping my bags at my feet, I take the offered cut. Holding it out in front of me, I read the word Prospect stitched on the back. Without wasting time, I slide it on.

"So, it begins," Jake states. "First things first. I need to speak with you in my office. Leave your shit at the bar. You can get settled after we talk." Without a word, I follow Jake down the hall to his office. I wait for him to take a seat behind his desk before I follow suit sitting in a chair in front of him. Jake leans back in his chair and studies me for a moment while running his palm through his beard before he opens his mouth. "I'll be the first person to tell each of my men that your personal shit is your own until it fucks with my club. I'm also a man who believes in laying my cards on the table when needed. I want to ask you where you stand when it comes to William McGregor?"

For a split second, I'm taken aback by Jake's question.

"Don't look so surprised, kid. I know exactly who you and your father are. I'm the President of this club, Sam. Never doubt I don't know everything about anyone who steps through my doors," he says with certainty.

"I wasn't trying to keep who my father is a secret from the club," I say, shaking my head. "When I left Texas, I vowed never to look back."

"I know ya did, son. If I had thought any different, you wouldn't be sittin' across from me now wearin' that cut. But I have to ask. Have you talked to your dad recently?"

"Yes, sir. He has been more persistent in reaching out to me. I spoke with him briefly this morning. Our conversation was the same as it usually is. Him insisting I come home and me telling him it's never going to happen."

"I'm going to assume you don't know why he is more intent on riding your ass lately," Jake sighs.

"Not really. I've only spoken to my dad a handful of times over the past year."

Jake runs his hand over his face and leans forward in his chair, resting his elbows on his desk. "Two weeks ago, District Attorney McGregor officially announced his candidacy for Governor of Texas," Jake announces, dropping the bomb.

"Fuckin' hell," I hiss. "Well, that explains why he's so eager for me to come home. It's time for my father to do what he does best, and that's put on a show for the people of Texas. What better way than to have his son by his side while he plays the dutiful family man."

"Yeah, that sounds about right," Jake agrees. It's then it hits me why he wanted to talk. "Are you second guessing my being a part of the club? Because of whom my father is—of who I am? I wouldn't want my baggage to affect The Kings, Jake. I can't sit here and guarantee my father won't be a problem in the future."

Jake leans back in his chair and chuckles. "Do you take me for the kind of man that will let any motherfucker, including William McGregor, dictate how I run my club?"

"No, sir, I don't. But I also care too much about the people I surround myself with to risk it."

"It's that answer right there that tells me I'm making the right decision with you, Sam. Go on and get your shit. Your room is down the hall last room on the left. I want to see you out at the bar in ten. I need you to make a run." With those parting words, Jake stands and walks out of his office.

Thirty minutes later, I arrive at Charley's, Polson's local bar, to pick up Jake's order. The club is having a family party tonight, and Charley is who the club orders their booze from.

"How's it hangin', Sam?" Charley asks as he steps out from behind the bar. "You here for the club?"

"Yes, sir. Everything ready for me?"

"Sure is kid. Come on back." He ushers me through the double doors leading to the back of the bar.

"Thanks, Charley."

Once I have finished loading the truck, I head back inside to deliver the envelope Jake sent with me to give Charley. The moment I step inside, I hear Charley arguing with some drunk. The first thing I notice about the guy is he's not a regular. He's not someone I've seen in town before. The guy stands at around 5 feet 11 inches and has a husky build. "Look, fella. Like I told you before. I don't offer tabs to non-locals. You don't like how I run my bar, you can get the hell out," Charley informs the man.

"I said I'm good for it. Now give me my fucking drink old man," the newcomer sneers.

"Is there a problem here?" I ask, stepping up to the bar. I know Charley is more than capable of taking care of himself, but I represent the club now, and Charley is under the protection of The Kings. I don't feel right leaving without knowing the situation is taken care of. Any one of the guys would do the same.

The man arguing with Charley turns in his seat at the sound of my voice. "Mind your own goddamn business."

Shaking my head, I eye Charley. Drunks are some of the most challenging people to deal with. "Sorry, man. Time to go," Charley orders, his tone indicating he's lost his patience.

Grabbing the guy's arm, I go to pull him from the stool. "Let's go, man." Pushing off from the bar, he snatches his arm from my grip and makes a move to punch my face. I grew up dodging my father's fists, so I can see the move from a mile away. Well, I was dodging them until I hit a growth spurt at sixteen and suddenly had five inches on my dad. Pairing my height with what football and working did to my physique had my father thinking twice about knocking me around. Blocking his fist, I counteract by bringing my left hand to the back of his head and slamming his face into the bar, causing the guy to howl in pain. I then fist his hair and raise his face to mine. I get a sick sense of satisfaction when I see blood seeping from his busted nose. "I'm going to ask you one more time. Do we have a problem here?"

"No. No problem here," he grinds out through clenched teeth. The moment I release him, the man wipes his face with the back of his hand, and for a second, I think he's going to square off with me again. When he cuts his eyes over to Charley holding a shotgun, he thinks better of it, leaving without another word.

When I return to the clubhouse, Logan is outside waiting on me. "Heard you ran into some trouble?"

"I did. It wasn't anything I couldn't handle, though."

"You make anything of the guy?"

I shake my head. "I think he was just someone passing through. Typical drunk."

"Alright. Keep your eyes open around town just in case," Logan warns.

"Will do," I say, lowering the tailgate of my truck.

"When you get done here, the bathrooms need cleanin'. Also,

the grass out back needs cut." Logan informs as he retreats inside the clubhouse. "Oh, one more thing," he says, looking over his shoulder with a smirk. "The riding mower is on the fritz. You'll have to cut it with the push. Don't worry; it's only ten thousand square feet."

After unloading the truck, cleaning the bathrooms in the clubhouse, including the ones in the guy's rooms, making a last-minute run to the store for Lisa, and cutting the grass while Logan and Gabriel were all too helpful on pointing out the spots I'd missed, I'm now headed to my room for a much-needed shower before the party. I was told the old ladies and children would be here. With hopes of seeing my Firefly tonight, I step into my room, shutting the door behind me. Sliding my cut off, I hang it on the back of the chair next to the bed, then pull my t-shirt off over my head and toss it in the dirty clothes basket. Retrieving my phone from my pocket, I go to fire off a text to Sofia only to be interrupted by another call from my dad. "Hello," I answer without hiding my annoyance.

"I'm through playing games with you, Sam. I want you on the next flight home."

"Not happening. I am home. Sorry dad, but you don't get to use me to further your career. You're going to have to figure out how to get the Governor's seat without me. Tell everyone I'm dead for all I care. Play the mournful father just like you did when mom died."

"Jesus Christ, Sam. Not this shit again. Your mother was a sick woman. I did the best I could by her."

"If you call slapping her around and cheating on her every chance you got doing right by her." I let the sarcasm fall out of my mouth. "Look. I'm not in the mood to take a stroll down memory lane and point out all the things that make you a shitty father. You calling me is pointless."

"Alright, son. Don't say I didn't warn you." The next thing I hear is a click letting me know the call has ended.

"Fucking prick," I mutter, tossing my phone on the bed. Determined not to let my father ruin my good mood, I continue with the task of getting ready for tonight's party. Snatching my duffle bag from the floor next to my feet, I heft it up onto the bed, unzip it and pull out a pair of clean jeans and a black t-shirt. Fishing around at the bottom of the bag, I pull out the 5x7 picture I have tucked underneath my clothes. The picture is of Sofia. It was taken last year while we were standing out by the lake at Logan's house during one of the kid's birthday parties. She was wearing a yellow sundress that complimented her honey color eyes perfectly. Her flawless skin was makeup-free aside from the cherry red lip gloss she loves to wear. I remember not being able to take my eyes off her. Over the past couple of years, I have been taking things with Sofia slow and steady. I don't know the details of her past, but my gut tells me it's tragic. That it's something that will have me wanting to kill the person who hurt her. I hope, in time, she will trust me enough to tell me her story. As of now, our friendship is solid. It has always been my intention to have a solid foundation with Sofia before moving things further. Although I have never really hidden my true feelings from her. I am always careful not to take things too far. What my Firefly may not know is I have been slowly getting her used to my touch and the idea of us. Sometimes it's me brushing my palm down her arm when we are standing close to one another, and sometimes it is me running my knuckles down her soft cheek when she's telling me about her day. Or when I lean in close to whisper in her ear how beautiful she is. I'll watch her pupils dilate and her breathing hitch as her warm breath dances across my face.

Closing my eyes, I groan when I feel my dick swell against my zipper. Popping the button on my jeans, I reach inside and free my aching cock. "Fuck," I hiss when I fist my erection and begin to pump. Thoughts of Sofia always lead me here. Knowing I'm going to see my Firefly tonight has me hard as a rock. Using my precum as lubrication, I close my eyes and jack off to visions of Sofia. It only takes a few minutes before I'm shooting my load all over my hand. Never in my life have I jacked off as much as I have since I laid eyes on Sofia.

Fifteen minutes later, I'm showered and ready for the party. Picking the picture of my girl off the bed, I walk over to the dresser, open the top drawer and place it inside. Grabbing my cut from the back of the chair, I slide it on over my black t-shirt, and I have to admit I love the weight of the leather on my shoulders. Looking down at my watch, I see we have a couple more hours before people will start to arrive, and I need to get busy. I'm sure the guys have a list of shit for me to do. When I appear from the hallway into the main room, I'm met by Jake, Gabriel, Reid, and Nikolai.

"Alba took Leah shopping today. I'm sure my woman will be draggin' that girl here tonight," Gabriel tells Jake. The mention of Leah reminds me of what I needed to talk to Jake about. I reach the bar where the guys are seated just as Jake speaks up. "I don't know why Alba forces that girl to come here. The poor thing is afraid of her own damn shadow. Being around all us men makes her unease even worse."

"Yeah, but it's not without good cause," I say, sitting down on a stool at the end of the bar.

Jake sighs. "No, I guess not."

"Since we are on the subject of Leah, I wanted to bring up a concern I have about her." I notice my statement catches Nikolai's attention.

"What is it, son?" Jake asks.

"I'm not feeling right about her staying alone. I know the apartment has top-notch security, and she has assured me she's fine with living by herself, but my gut says she's not ready. I promised my friend I'd take care of her. So, I'm coming to the club in hopes you all can help me figure out a solution to not only keep Leah safe but to make her feel safe."

Just as Jake goes to open his mouth, Nikolai steps forward with a look on his face I can't decipher. "I'll be taking care of Leah." Just as quick as Nikolai makes his declaration, he turns on his heel and walks out of the clubhouse. Jake then turns to me with a grin that matches my own.

"Problem solved."

4

SOFIA

"Do you think she'll be ready to come out of her room this morning?" Emma says, sitting on the chair across from me. Pulling the butter toward her, she spreads some onto her toast.

"I hope so," I tell her as I squeeze extra honey into my mug then stir it. "Dr. Kendrick said she reads lips extremely well, so communicating with her shouldn't be a problem. If we give her time, she'll open up." Looking out the window, I spot Sam along with Reid standing at a makeshift table with a large sheet of paper spread out before them.

"You like him?" Emma asks.

Tearing my eyes off Sam, I pull apart the chocolate croissant sitting on the small white saucer in front of me. Taking a bite from the center of the pastry, I feel Emma studying me. Still chewing on my food, I lift my eyes to see her waiting for my reply with a smile on her face. Tearing off another piece, I grin then pop another bite in my mouth, trying to avoid giving her an answer.

"It's sweet how he looks at you and how he brings you breakfast every morning." She casts her eyes down to her plate and pushes what is left of her scrambled eggs around her plate with the fork in her hand. "I want someone to look at me like that." The longing in her voice pulls at my heart.

"You will, Emma. Someday, someone worthy of you will come along and love you the way you deserve to be loved." I do my best to reassure her. Feeling the need to lighten the mood, I mention the fact she got the job yesterday. "So, are you excited to be starting your new job at the library today?"

"More than ready. I was so nervous walking through those doors yesterday, but Mrs. Davis, the head Librarian, put me at ease right away. Just another step toward finding myself again, right?" Pushing herself from the table, Emma stands, takes her plate to the sink, rinses it, and places her dish inside the dishwasher. Getting up, I do the same. My shift at work starts in an hour, and I always like to get there a little early. "Well," Emma slings her purse over her right shoulder, "I'm off to work."

"See you later." I smile at her over my shoulder. I'm still standing at the kitchen sink when I feel someone behind me. Spinning around, I spot Luna standing quietly just inside the kitchen door, and I smile at her. She looks to be in her early twenties. She is about the same height as me but a little curvier. She has long, beautiful blonde hair, but it's her eyes that stand out the most. I've never seen someone with violet eyes before. "Hi," I say. Wiping my hands dry with a hand towel, I walk up to her. "Nice to finally meet you; I'm Sofia."

After studying me for a moment, her face relaxes, and she gives me a small smile in return. Then using sign language, she starts to communicate with me. I feel terrible because I don't understand what she's trying to tell me. Just as quickly, she realizes this and pulls a small notebook from the pocket of her sweater. From the same pocket, she retrieves a pen and begins to write. Handing me the notebook, I read.

Good morning. Sorry for not introducing myself last night. My name is Luna.

Handing her notebook over, I make sure I'm looking at her when I speak so she can easily read my lips. "That's okay. I get it. New place and all. Would you like some coffee?" I wait for her to write another response to the paper.

I would love some.

I motion toward the table for her to sit. After fixing her drink, I place the steaming mug in front of her, and she looks up at me. "What do you like in your coffee?"

Sliding the notebook over I read, *I like it cold—milk, sugar, and ice.*

Turning, I head toward the refrigerator, fill a cup with ice cubes, grab the milk, and on my way back, snag the sugar bowl from beside the breadbox with a teaspoon. I notice the time showing on the microwave. Placing my hand lightly on Luna's shoulder getting her attention while she scoops a spoonful of sugar into the hot coffee, I tell her, "Will you be okay until Dr. Kendrick comes by? I have to go to work." Her eyes glance toward the French doors where she can see the men milling about in the backyard then glances back at me. "Don't worry about them. They are not allowed to enter the house, and I promise I will lock the doors." Looking a little unsure, she begins to write again. This time I notice her hand shaking a little as the tip of the pen glides across the paper. Just as she goes to hand me her note, I hear the security bell chime, which lets me know someone has entered the home.

How long will I be alone?

"Not long. I promise. And, there are only five people outside this house that have the code to get in here." Just as I get those words from my mouth, Mila calls out my name.

"Sofia!"

"In the kitchen!" I call back. Luna relaxes and slumps her body against the back of the chair. Closing her eyes, she takes in a deep breath. Looking at me again, she writes the word *sorry,* and her eyes glaze over. "Never apologize for being afraid," I tell her, continuing to hold her stare until Mila walks into the kitchen with her arms loaded down with shopping bags.

"Hey." She pauses, taking in the scene. "Everything okay?" She walks across the tiled floor and places her bags on the counter.

I look back at Mila. "Everything is okay." Facing Luna, I give her hand one more reassuring squeeze and introduce them to one another. "Luna, this is Mila." Mila comes and stands beside me. "Mila, meet Luna."

"So good to meet you. Dr. Kendrick called me last night and said you might need a few personal things, so I stopped by the store. If you don't mind spending your morning with me, we can go through everything," Mila asks her with a friendly smile. Once Luna replies with a nod, I feel confident in leaving the house.

With a small wave, I leave the two of them in the kitchen. Entering my room, I grab my bag off the hook on my wall and the keys to my yellow fully customized four-door Volkswagen Beetle off the top of my dresser. The car was a gift from The Kings for my twentieth birthday just over a month ago.

With my car parked inside the security of the garage, I walk back through the kitchen where Mila and Luna have clothes, shoes, and makeup scattered all over the kitchen table. Mila looks up. "Don't forget about the party this evening."

With my hand on the door handle, I glance over my shoulder. "I'll be there." Sliding into the driver's seat of my car, I toss my bag on the passenger seat. Pressing the button above my head, the garage door opens, flooding the space around me with sunlight. Backing out, I pause, and as the garage door closes, I let the top down on my car.

I don't ride a motorcycle as The Kings and Sam do, but I imagine the feeling they get with the sun on their skin and the wind in their hair is the same I get when I drive with my car top down—alive and free.

. . .

PULLING into the parking lot of The Pier, I spot Carol setting out a large chalkboard that advertises the specials of the day. She waves in my direction as I park in my usual spot close to the building.

"Good morning, sweetie." Carol greets me with a warm embrace the moment I reach the last step onto the massive wrap around deck connecting to a long dock right over the bay. "You look beautiful as always. Come on inside; we have a busy day ahead of us. The week-long festival on the bay starts today, which means we will have double the customers all week long."

I've been hearing about this event since living here in Polson but have never experienced it. And being I didn't start working here for Carol until after the events took place last year, I have no idea what to expect. Polson's 34th annual Party on the Bay lasts an entire week. From what I know, boaters take part in onshore fun and games as well as car shows, boat shows, and a 5k charity run. People from all over Montana come in to take part. The only part I got the chance to experience last year was the fireworks show at the end of the week. A group of us from school, along with Leah and Sam, watched the show from the end of the dock right here. That was the summer I started looking at Sam in a different light.

Wow. Carol wasn't lying when she said we would be busy today. The lunch rush was triple our usual amount. Running my fingers through my hair, I twist it around itself, forming a loose bun and securing it with a few bobby pins I retrieved from my bag in the breakroom. I look up from untying my apron strings when Amy, Carol's daughter, who has become my best friend, walks in.

"Hey, Sof. Ready for our lunch break?" She tosses her apron into her locker. Amy is the one who helped me get the waitressing job here.

"More than ready."

Going to the kitchen, Amy and I fill our cups full of cold fresh cherry limeade and grab a couple of baskets of chicken poppers with fries. Taking our lunch outside, we walk to the end of the dock.

"You want to come out with Ben, and I tonight? We're going to hang out at the bowling alley?" Amy asks.

I pop a fry in my mouth. "The club is having a family party tonight. Besides, I don't want to be the third wheel on your date." I swing my legs as they dangle over the edge.

"You're not a third wheel, Sof."

Tossing a fry into the water, I watch as two fish pick at it from beneath the surface of the water.

"Maybe next time then. You should invite Sam too." She playfully nudges me with her shoulder.

Giving her an eye roll, I tell her, "Sam has better things to do than have me drag him to the bowling alley."

Amy sighs. "Sof, Sam would do anything you ask him to do. That man seriously adores you."

Amy doesn't understand why I hesitate to form an actual relationship with Sam. She sees his affection for me, and I've confided in her that I like him, but I haven't been able to bring myself to tell him how I feel, though I suspect he already knows. Amy knows that I have been through something in my past, but I've never talked with her about it before, and I'm not sure if I ever will. I know talking about it is a good thing and that it may help empower others to speak their truth as well, but it can be difficult. There is a massive vulnerability in showing those types of unseen scars to the world. What I went through was not my fault. I know that. It's fear of how others in this world may look at me after they find out.

We sit there quietly for several minutes as we munch on our food. In the distance, I watch the boaters enjoying this beautiful day without a care in the world.

"You ready to get back to it for another three hours?" Amy shoves her leftovers in her bag, stands, and chucks it into the trash bin nearby. Placing my uneaten food into the paper bag, I roll the top down. Lending a hand, Amy pulls me to my feet.

Sensing my mood has shifted, Amy keeps hold of my hand, swinging our arms back and forth between us as we begin to walk back toward the restaurant. "Remember last summer at the fair when you sat on a melted chocolate ice cream cone?" She laughs.

"I looked like I sat in caca, that was not funny." I start laughing along with her, and just like that, my best friend makes me smile.

"Yeah, but you didn't let that stop you from having fun," she says, making her point loud and clear.

"Thanks, Amy."

"That's what friends are for."

A FEW HOURS LATER, I'm pulling up to the clubhouse. Laughter can be heard coming from the back of the property, and the smell of food cooking on the grill permeates the air around me. The Kings throw parties, mostly family gatherings more than anything, almost any chance they get. Besides the brotherhood, the family is the core foundation amongst them all, and to them, I am a part of that.

As I'm reaching in the backseat for the sheet cake, Carol helped me bake today; I'm startled by a voice. "Hey there, darlin'." Clutching my chest, I spin around. "Shit. Sorry, Sofia, I didn't mean to scare ya. Here, let me grab that cake for you." Quinn says, lifting the cardboard lid.

"Don't stick your finger in the frosting," I fuss the moment his finger is about to swipe some of the icing from the corner.

"What kind of cake is this?" Quinn closes the lid.

"Chocolate cake with chocolate buttercream icing."

"My favorite," he says as I walk beside him, heading toward the backyard.

Throwing my head back, I laugh. "Every cake is your favorite, Quinn."

"You make it?" he asks.

"Yep." I beam.

"Then today it's my favorite." He gives me his megawatt smile.

Rounding the corner of the building, Bella's daughter Breanna spots me and makes a beeline in my direction. "Sofi, Sofi, Sofi!" She giggles as she calls my name. With outstretched arms, I scoop her up.

"Hey, munchkin. You having fun?"

"Yep." Breanna smiles. I adore her. I love all the kids in my big crazy adopted family. Squeezing my neck, Breanna wiggles free wanting to join the other kids again. I scan the yard noticing everyone but Leah has arrived, but to be honest, I'm searching for one person in particular—Sam.

"Sofia." Bella waves, catching my attention. Her and the other women are sitting in adirondack chairs around the fire pit. Crossing the lawn, I join them.

"Hey guys." I wave to them, then sink into one of two empty chairs next to Alba.

"You look tired," Alba mentions, taking a sip of her drink.

"Yeah. The first day of Party on the Bay festivities," I tell her.

"You know, we were all thinking of signing up for the 5k run. The charity they are giving to is our very own New Hope House," Mila announces.

I lean forward in my seat. "Really?"

"Mhmm." Mila sips her wine. "We've been trying to talk the guys into doing it too."

"How'd that go?" I giggle, knowing the outcome a conversation like that would be like. Not that The Kings don't want to give back. Those men do a lot for this community.

Alba laughs. "The only response I got from Gabriel was a grunt." We all laugh with her.

I watch Logan approach walking behind Bella's chair. Tugging on her ponytail, he tips her head back and kisses her. "You ladies need another round of drinks? It looks like you could use some more wood on the fire as well." Turning, he shouts across the yard to Quinn. "Hey, Quinn, tell Sam the ladies need drinks!"

"You got it!" Quinn calls out.

Logan looks my way. "What do you want, sweetheart?"

"Soda is fine," I tell him.

Yelling, he tells Quinn, "Sofia wants a soda. Tell him to restock the fridge if it's low too!" Looking back at his woman, Logan tells her, "Give me your lips, Angel. Reid and Quinn are almost done with the grilling, so I'm gonna start setting out tables and chairs." Leaning her head back one more time, Bella waits for Logan to kiss her.

Moments later, Sam is striding toward us with a cooler in one hand and several blocks of wood for the fire under his other arm. Our eyes lock, sending those familiar butterflies in my stomach fluttering about. It's not until he sets the cooler on the ground next to Grace and starts placing the logs in the fire do I realize what he is wearing. A leather cut just like the rest of the men except with no logo. Only one patch. The single word Prospect on the bottom. I'm speechless. *When did this happen?*

Once the fire is to his liking, Sam makes eye contact with me again. "Shit, I forgot your drink," he says, and jogs back toward the house.

I look around at all the women. "Sam is prospecting?"

Emerson gets up from her chair, opens the cooler, and starts passing drinks around. "Yep, and I think he will make a great member." The others nod in agreement.

As Sam approaches, he pops the top of the can and hands it to me. Our fingertips touch sending electric currents coursing through them. It causes my heart to race. "Thank you."

"You're welcome, Firefly." The use of his nickname makes me

smile. Turning, Sam leaves, going over to help Logan and Reid set the tables.

Closing my eyes, I sink back in my chair. When I open them, Bella, Alba, Mila, Grace, and Emerson are all staring at me—all wearing smiles on their faces.

"What?" Bringing the can to my lips, I take another sip hoping they let it go for now, which they do because Alba begins talking about the 5k run.

"So, are we going to commit to this charity run?" Alba chimes in.

One by one, all of them agree to do it, which leaves me. Anything for a good cause, especially our foundation will always be a yes, so I tell them, "Count me in too."

Dinner is announced shortly after, and I help the women wrangle the kids up and get them seated with plates of food before we fix ours and sit down. "Sam, why didn't Leah come with you?" I ask as he sits next to me at the end of the table.

"I stopped by the apartment when I went out for some ice, and she said she wasn't feeling well," he informs me with a knowing look. Sam knew she wasn't telling the truth, but he never pushes.

I take a big bite of the flavorful Cuban dish Ropa Vieja that Alba made. With conversation flowing amongst everyone, I finally get around to asking Sam about the whole prospect thing. "So—prospect, huh?"

Sam's shoulders shake as he chuckles. "I'm surprised you lasted this long before asking me about it, Firefly. Anyway, the club approached me about it, and they think I have potential. The Kings stand for everything I believe in; a brotherhood and what a family should be. There is no doubt I believe I am right where I belong."

"You'll make a great King, Sam," I confess.

"That means a lot coming from you, Firefly."

Dinner is over before we know it, and the sun has disappeared behind the trees. Sitting near the firepit on a large log used for seating, I watch the fireflies twinkle as they hover just above the ground while listening to the guys cut up behind me and their women laugh along with them. Tired and ready for bed, I decide I need to head back to my place before it gets too late. Standing, I turn and face everyone. "I'm heading to the house. I have work again tomorrow."

Jake glances over at Sam. "Escort Sofia home." Nodding, Sam stands, and we walk side by side around the edge of the building. Stopping at my car, Sam opens my door and waits for me to settle in and buckle before closing it for me.

"Is this all part of your prospect duties?" I tease, knowing he would follow me home anyway. He always does.

"I'm right behind you, beautiful." Mounting his bike, the one he's had for a while now, Sam waits for me to start my car. I pull away from the compound, and he falls in behind me. It's at least a thirty-minute drive from the clubhouse to my place. I look out at the flat open land as we drive down the road. Darkness is setting as the horizon swallows the sun putting another day to bed, leaving the sky painted in rich, deep purple and blue hues which fade to black as it reaches the stars.

BEFORE LONG, I'm pulling into the driveway and parking in the garage. Like always, I wait for Sam to walk the outside perimeter before getting out of the car. Knowing he also checks the inside of the house, I hand over my keys and follow him in as the garage door slowly lowers. I watch him as he moves about the house. Something is different about him tonight. The way he carries himself is different. The way he moves. *He has more confidence, maybe?*

Maybe it's not him at all.

Maybe it's me.

He looks good wearing that cut. Looking away before he catches me, I cross the living room and wait by the front door.

"Have lunch with me tomorrow?"

"I have to work," I tell him.

"I'll come to you."

Butterflies fill my stomach again when he brushes a strand of hair away from my face. "Okay," I agree.

"Lock up behind me."

Opening the door, Sam steps out on the front porch. Knowing he won't budge until hearing the locks engage, I slowly close the door. With the deadbolts locked and the alarm reset, I listen to the rumble of his Harley and wait for the sound to fade away before heading to my bedroom. The house is quiet, and the lights are off in both Emma and Luna's room. After changing into my PJ's and going down the hall to the bathroom to wash my face and brush my teeth, I lock my bedroom door and climb into bed. The last thought I have before falling asleep—Sam.

5

SAM

"I'm sorry you had to come out here just to bring me some milk, Sam," Alba grumbles as she strolls down the steps of her front porch. "It's five in the morning for Christ's sake. Gabriel could have gotten up to run to the store," she continues to fuss when she reaches me, and I chuckle.

"It's not a big deal, Alba," I say, climbing off my bike and pulling two half gallons of milk from the saddlebag. "Don't go getting upset on my behalf, little momma. I knew what was to be expected of me the moment I accepted the prospect cut."

"I don't like seeing my friend treated like a slave," she pouts.

"I'm not being treated as a slave. You're looking at things the wrong way. Any task given to me by the guys is allowing me to prove my service to the club. I need to show them I am willing to go above and beyond. I have to demonstrate my commitment." Cocking my head to the side, I ask, "Have you witnessed the guys asking me to do anything they wouldn't do at any given time?"

Alba seems to ponder my question a moment then answers, "No."

"Do you get it now?"

"Yeah, I get it. I guess this is all just a little weird for me."

"I get that. But Alba—" I pause until she looks directly in my eyes. "This," I say, tugging on my prospect cut, "is what I want."

"I understand, Sam. The club, this family, they're all pretty amazing. I'm happy for you. I'm glad you have been able to find yourself here." Shaking her head, Alba lets out a snort. "I'll admit I would never have thought."

"There are a lot of things about me people would have never thought," I grin. "It's easy for people to assume." At my last statement, I cock my head with a lifted brow. Alba blushes because she knows exactly what I'm referring to.

"Yeah, I'm sorry about the whole gay thing, Sam. It's just that day in the coffee shop a few days after we met, I saw the way you were looking at that couple; at the guy."

"Yeah, well, when you wake up one morning after a night of drinking, and you're laying butt ass naked in a bed next to a dude and a chick you don't know and have no recollection of what the hell went down the night before; then see them months later sittin' across from us in a coffee shop, things tend to be awkward," I deadpan. If I thought Alba couldn't turn redder than she already was, I was wrong. Her embarrassment makes me chuckle. Letting her off the hook, I decide to take my leave. I have to be at work soon, anyway. I kiss the top of her head. "See ya later, little momma."

"Bye, Sam. Thanks for the milk," she says, making her way back toward the house. Climbing on my bike, I spot Gabriel as he steps out onto the front porch. I tip my head, and he does the same just before I start my bike and pull out of the driveway.

After leaving Alba and Gabriel's place, I made my usual stop at the bakery and headed to Sofia's. On the ride there, I take the time to reflect on the many changes I have faced since leaving Texas and how the choices I have made have led me to this point in my life. When I left home after high school, I was a boy whose father had mapped his future out for him and was expected to attend law school so he could take over the family firm. The McGregor law firm is one of the most well-known and respected firms in Texas. My grandfather started it nearly forty years ago and still practices to this day. My father, of course, followed in his footsteps, and from day one, I was to do the same. My leaving Texas and refusing to go to law school was not some sort of rebellious phase. It was me keeping a promise I made to my mother long ago. My mom knew I was meant for something different. She made me promise to go out in the world and find what that was. My only problem is both my father and grandfather are ruthless in business and are known not to take no for an answer. That's how I know he won't stop until he gets what he wants from me. Although I think it's more about me telling him no than him needing me. The question is, what does William McGregor have planned?

When I get to New Hope House, I'm not surprised to see Sofia already up. She's an early riser. This morning she is sitting on the back deck. Next to her is a young woman with blonde hair. When I climb the steps of the porch, I immediately notice the blonde's unease and halt my advance. I watch as Sofia picks up a notebook and pen off the table beside her and scribbles on paper before she passes it to the woman. The blonde's eyes flicker from the note to Sofia then back to me. When she offers a smile, I take that as an okay to continue up the porch. "Miss," I greet the young woman. I turn to Sofia and hand her the bag with pastries. "Good morning, Firefly." I bend down and brush my lips across her cheek.

"Good morning, Sam." She blushes.

"Are we still on for lunch today?" I ask, and she nods.

"Good. I'll see ya then, baby." I don't miss the way her eyes go big when the word baby rolls off my tongue. It's the first time I've called her that. It's the next step in my plan to make her mine, and the way her breath hitches tells me she likes it.

"Okay," she breathes.

Over the next several hours, my focus is on finishing the frame for the sixth bedroom on the New Hope House addition. I have a crew coming out tomorrow to begin laying sheetrock. When I look over my shoulder, I notice one of the guys is missing. I turn to James. "You see where Dylan went?" James has been with Kings Construction almost as long as me and is one of the best workers on my crew. Dylan, on the other hand, is a slacker. I have to constantly ride his ass for him to get anything done. I've spoken to Reid and Nikolai about him. They both gave me permission to can his ass if need be. I'm trying to give the guy a chance, but his disappearing acts don't sit well with me. "I saw him over by the shed earlier taking a smoke break," James informs.

Walking around the side of the house and over to the small shed at the edge of the property, I find the motherfucker with his ass propped against the structure, scrolling through his phone and a cigarette hanging from his mouth. I have officially had it with him. "Yo. Break time is over. Pack your shit and get the hell out of here. You're done." Cutting my eyes down to the ground where Dylan stands, I grind my teeth when I see a shit ton of cigarette butts littering the area.

"Oh. Hey man," Dylan says, tucking his phone in his pocket. "I was taking a little break. Don't get bent out of shape about it." He shrugs, tossing his half-smoked cigarette to the ground. Dylan goes to move around me as if he didn't hear me tell his dumbass he was done. Reaching out, I grab his bicep. "Pick them up," I grind out, looking him dead in his eyes.

"Pick what up?" he shrugs from my hold.

I gesture to the ground at his feet. "The butts. Pick them up."

"Are you fucking serious, man?"

"Hell yeah, I'm serious. Pick that shit up. You don't disrespect someone else's property by coming onto it and leaving your trash behind. Especially not here. Now pick that shit up and take it with you. You're done here." Something in my tone must tell Dylan not to test me because he does what he's told and leaves. "Fuckin' tool," I mutter.

Meeting up with Sofia for lunch, I pull into the parking lot at The Pier and climb off my bike the same moment she steps out of the front entrance. My heart and my dick swell at how indescribably beautiful she is. By the time we reach each other, I can't hold back my smile as she shyly beams from ear to ear. Using both palms, I cup her silky-smooth face and kiss her forehead. "Hey, baby."

"Hi. I got our lunch." She holds up a white paper bag. "Burgers and fries, okay?"

"Yeah, Firefly. Burgers sound good." I grab her hand. "Come on." I lead Sofia to the end of the dock to eat. It's her favorite spot out here. We enjoy our lunch in comfortable silence for a few minutes while staring out at the water before she speaks up.

"What's on your mind, Sam?" she asks, popping a fry into her mouth. I watch completely hypnotized by her pouty lips as she chews her food. Leaning in, I use the pad of my thumb to swipe the bit of ketchup from the corner of her mouth. She watches me as I bring the same thumb to my mouth, licking the ketchup from it. Her eyes go from my mouth to my heated stare. Knocking herself from her stupor, she clears her throat. "Are you going to answer my question?"

Balling up my trash, I shove it into the bag. "My dad is giving me shit."

"What do you mean?"

"He wants me to come home." My heart aches with the devastated look that crosses my Firefly's face when I mention leaving.

"Are you? Are you going back home?" she stammers while looking down at her lap.

Placing my finger under her chin, I bring Sofia's gorgeous eyes to mine. "I am home. Nothing in this world could ever make me leave Polson or you, Firefly. Never." Sofia visibly relaxes at my declaration. Not wanting the subject of my father ruining our time together, I change the subject. "The guys said they were taking their old ladies to the festival this evening."

"Yeah, I heard that too. I was thinking about going."

"Good. That means you'll be on the back of my bike then." Standing, I hold out my hand. Without hesitation, Sofia takes it, and I help her stand. "I'll pick you up at 4:00."

After work, I stop by Kings Construction to turn in an order form for next week's materials for New Hope House. I knock on Reid's office door. "Hey, you got a minute?"

"Yeah. Come on in," Reid nods toward the chair in front of his desk.

"I wanted to drop off my order for next week."

"No problem." He takes the form from my hand. "I heard what happened with Dylan."

"Yeah?"

Reid nods. "His pansy ass came in here whinin' after you sent him on his way. I told him what's done is done. You gave the fucker too many chances. More than most people would. Did you really make him pick up his cigarette butts?" He chuckles.

"Hell yeah," I laugh and stand as Reid does the same.

"Let's get the hell out of here. Mila will have my ass if I'm late. You coming out to the festival tonight?"

"Yeah. I'm going to head to the clubhouse now and change before I go pick up my girl." Reid raises a brow at the mention of me referring to Sofia as my girl but says nothing. At this point, they all know. Things aren't official yet. But they will be.

Making our way out to our bikes, I climb on mine the same time Reid straddles his. With a nod, he takes off in the opposite direction toward his and Mila's place while I head to the clubhouse.

I'm knocking on Sofia's door an hour later, and when she

answers, I swallow my tongue. She has on a pair of short white cut-off shorts and a yellow v-neck t-shirt that shows a tiny sliver of skin at her waistline. She's paired her outfit with bronze-colored sandals. The look is simple, yet she makes it look sexy as hell. "You look beautiful, baby."

Sofia ducks her head. "Thank you."

"Get your stuff, Firefly," I say, my tone husky.

Peeking up through her lashes, she nods and reaches to her left, grabbing her purse that's hanging on the hook just inside the front door. Sliding her bag over her shoulder, she takes my offered hand as I lead her to my bike. She waits for me to straddle my bike first before climbing on behind me. Once she's settled with her hands at my sides, I decide she is not close enough for my liking. Reaching behind me, I clutch underneath her knees and pull her flush against my back. I then bring her arms around my waist, settling her palms against my abdomen. Carefully, I gauge her reaction to being so close to me. It's a bold and risky move on my part, but my gut tells me she's ready. I'm always careful with each movement, with each step I take with Sofia. When her body relaxes and melds into mine, I know she is okay with the move. Squeezing her hand, I glance over my shoulder and wink.

The drive to the festival is a short one, but because I'm selfish and want the feel of my girl on the back of my bike a little longer, I take a long route there. I'm sure Sofia knows what I'm doing but says nothing. I'm hoping it's because she's as content at the moment as I am.

"There they are." She points over my shoulder to where the guys have gathered and are standing around with the women. Parking my bike next to the group, Sofia climbs off and makes her way over to Bella and Alba, giving them both a hug.

"I'm so glad you guys came." Bella smiles. "What should we do first?"

"I say we head on over to the pavilion and grab a couple of

beers first," Logan suggests. "Lord knows we're going to need it tonight." Next to him, Gabriel grunts in agreement.

"It's going to be fun. Just wait and see." Bella playfully swats Logan's arm.

"I'm going to find a bathroom," Sofia chimes in. "I'll meet everyone there."

"I'll go with you."

"You don't have to do that, Sam. I'll be okay," Sofia insists.

Shaking my head, I tell her, "No. I'll take you." I turn to the group. "We'll be on in a minute." The guys give me a look of approval as we head in separate directions.

I'm standing outside the restaurant where Sofia went in to use the restroom when a chick with bleach blonde hair and a shit ton of makeup on her face comes sauntering in my direction with an exaggerated sway to her hips. She and her friend have been eye-fucking me the past couple of minutes, and I knew one of them was bound to approach me; even though nothing about the look on my face says I'm interested.

"Hi there," the blonde says, batting her eyelashes.

Sighing, I give her my attention. "Not interested."

"Oh, come on now. You look like you're here for a good time. We can have some fun together. Maybe take me back to your clubhouse."

Jesus fucking Christ. This must be what the guys were talking about when they said a lot of women come into town looking to hook up with a biker. "It's not going to happen—get lost." It's not like me to be so rude to a female, but I'll be damned if my girl comes out here and is faced with this shit. Sofia's feelings are the only ones that matter right now. The blonde sneers, turns her nose in the air, and totters back over toward her friend. A beat later, Sofia appears from inside the restaurant.

"Thanks for waiting for me."

"I'd wait forever for you, Firefly."

As we push through the crowd, I notice Sofia's unease. Over to our right, I spot an alleyway that I know cuts through the block supplying a shortcut to the pavilion. Tugging on her hand, I lead us down the alley.

Once we are about halfway down the alley, a voice calls out behind us. "Look who the fuck we have here." Turning, I see three guys. One is the same man that was kicked out of Charley's the other day. "You remember me, asshole?" he taunts, strolling in mine and Sofia's direction. "Is this the guy who broke your nose, Johnny?" his friend asks.

"Sure as fuck is. I think the asshole needs a taste of his own medicine."

Sofia has a death grip on my hand, and a look of fear on her face as the three men continue their advance. Oh, hell, no. These motherfuckers don't realize just how bad they screwed up. Ushering my girl behind me, I stand to my full height. "It would be in your best interest to turn the fuck around and walk back the same way you came," I warn, my voice low and even. Turning to Sofia, I gesture for her to get out of here. Not heeding my warning, the guy whose nose I busted advances on me and takes a swing. Ducking, I avoid the punch. Instead, I deliver a solid blow to his gut, then bring my booted foot up to his chest and send him to the ground. Leaning over the man who is now laying flat on his back, the same man who dares scare my girl, I fist his shirt and deliver another blow to his face. "You piece of fuckin' shit," I seethe. Just as I raise my fist once again, I hear Sofia cry out behind me.

"Sam, look out!"

I turn just in time to see the man's buddy fly at my back. Before he has a chance to sucker punch me, Logan comes out of nowhere, tackling him to the ground.

6

SOFIA

Within seconds the rest of The Kings men arrive. Just as another man rushes in trying to peel Sam off his friend, Gabriel grabs the guy by the collar of his Polo shirt, yanking him back. His feet dangle as Gabriel lifts him a couple of inches off the ground before slamming his body to the ground, knocking the breath from the man's lungs. To my left, Logan hovers over the second man. My eyes shift back to Sam, who delivers a sharp blow to his target's rib cage bringing him to his knees. Immediately, Jake steps in. Clasping his hand over Sam's shoulder, he instructs him to stop. "That's enough, son."

I watch as Logan and Gabriel step back, allowing the guy's buddies to pick their battered friend off the ground by the arms, then watch them scuffle away, never looking back.

Once again, my eyes fall on Sam. Jake and the men are talking with him in hushed tones a couple of yards away. Jake's body partially obstructs his face as he stares at the ground, nodding a few times at whatever is being said to him. I've never seen Sam so angry. The moment he lifts his head, he zeros in on me. My eyes lock with his, and instantly, I watch his rage subside, and his expression softens as the tension leaves his body. Standing among the other women, Sam is the only person I focus on as he stalks toward me. My heart continues to race even though the confrontation with those men has ended. Stopping in front of me, Sam takes my face in the palms of his hands.

"You okay?" His touch calms my nerves yet lights my skin on fire at the same time.

I part my lips sucking in a breath. "I'm okay," I assure him.

"You sure?" He searches my eyes for the truth.

I nod. "Promise."

Someone's throat clears, snapping us both from the little bubble we've created. "Now, what do you say we get on that pontoon Quinn's dad loaned us for the night and get ready to watch the fireworks show?" Jake announces, grabbing Grace around her waist.

Sam glances down at me and grins before dropping his hands. Letting others lead the way we fall back a few steps behind them. "I'm sorry I put you in that situation back there, Firefly."

"They started it, Sam."

"The look on your face..." He pauses. "Fear. I don't like it beautiful. It won't happen again."

Doing something I never do, I slip my hand in his. "I knew you wouldn't let anything happen to me. I feel safe with you, Sam. I'm more relieved you're okay, and the other guys showed up when they did," I confess.

Silence falls between us as we walk along the pebbled shoreline on our way to the boat launch. The boat finally comes into view. Stopping, everyone boards the pontoon. After sitting down on the bench seat along the railing, Sam notices me shiver when the wind gusts.

"Be right back, babe." Turning, he strides toward Emerson, who's pulling out throw blankets from under the seat storage bin. Walking back with one, he drapes it across my shoulders.

"Thank you," I whisper as he sits beside me.

"You want a soda or some water? Mila packed a whole cooler of drinks along with some light snacks," Sam asks, and I shake my head. Wrapping his arm around me, he tucks me into his side. The warmth from his body has me closing my eyes for a moment.

"This is nice." My eyes pop open the moment I realize I spoke my mind out loud. I feel the heat rise in my cheeks. Chancing a quick peek in his direction, I catch him grinning, and my face flushes. Facing the setting sun, we sit in silence as Quinn maneuvers the boat out of the marina into the open waters of the bay.

Darkness eventually falls a short time later. Laughter and conversation flow naturally between Sam and me like it always does.

"So, have you heard anything from the admissions office yet about those online courses you wanted to start taking?" Sam inquires.

Keeping the blanket tucked around my shoulders, I shift my body to face his and press my back against the corner railing behind me. Slipping his hand behind my knees, he lifts my legs, slides a couple of inches down the bench, and brings them to rest across his lap.

"Not yet," I say with disappointment.

"I'm sure they will be in touch any day now."

The first set of fireworks lit up the night sky with a warm red and white glow as the sparks burst outward. Just as fast, another cluster of colorful explosions illuminates the sky. "Look at that one. How they get them to form shapes like that is amazing." My eyes fall to Sam's face. The heated stare he is giving me stokes the fire building deep inside my soul. "You're missing the show," I point toward the sky behind him.

Sam caresses my thigh just above my knee, causing my skin to prickle. I watch as his pupils dilate with the reaction my body has to his touch. "I'd much rather look at you." He leans in a bit closer. Biting my lower lip, I drop my eyes for a moment. Sam gently runs the back of his knuckles along my jawline before lifting my chin. My eyes lock with his. With our lips a breath apart, his fingertips tuck my fallen hair behind my ears. "You are beautiful." With my sharp inhale, the smell of Sam's woodsy cologne mixed with the leather from his cut invades all my senses. My heart races. My gaze drops to his lips, and I want so badly to feel them pressed against mine. I want to taste him. I want Sam to kiss me.

With his palm resting on the back of my neck, he whispers, "I want to kiss you, Firefly."

I want his lips on mine so badly I feel like I need his kiss to breathe. "I want that too." His lips descend upon mine. His lips are soft, and his kiss slow but steady. It was everything I could ask for in a real first kiss. The moment his mouth leaves mine, I feel dizzy. The way you feel when standing too fast.

Sam rests his forehead against mine. "Breathe, baby."

I feel silly when a small giggle escapes me. "I'm trying." Pulling back, he looks at me. "I've wanted to do that for so long," I whisper. "Thank you, Sam, for being patient with me all this time."

"You're worth waiting for, Firefly." Sam presses his lips to mine one more time.

"Hot damn. Fuck the fireworks. We have our damn show right here!" Quinn proclaims. Sam chuckles. I peek over his shoulder to find everyone watching us. They all start cheering, and I shake my head.

I smile at Sam. "I wouldn't trade them for all the money in the world."

THE FOLLOWING day I'm finding it difficult to focus. All I can think about is Sam and our kiss. How difficult it was to let him go after he brought me home last night. I find myself wanting to be on the back of his bike again with my arms wrapped tight around his waist with the wind in my hair and the sun on my face. Sitting here on the couch in the living room, I watch TV with Luna while I wait for Dr. Kendrick to arrive for my weekly session. Luna isn't watching the show. She's sketching in her journal. I never see her write words in it. Today it happens to be a beautiful drawing of a couple. The realism in her artwork makes it feel like the images will jump from the paper. Luna lifts her head and notices me watching her. "How do I sign the word beautiful?" I ask her.

Luna raises her hand, her palm facing her face, then spreads her fingers and makes a swiping motion like she's removing a mask. I repeat her actions a few times, making sure my moves are exact. Her smile and nod confirm I've done well. Pointing to the couple sketched on paper lying on her lap, I sign *beautiful.*

Ripping the page from her journal, she hands it to me. "Really? Are you sure?" I ask, and she nods. Lifting the paper, I look at it, taking in all the tiny details. Their faces look familiar. Realizing I'm staring at images of Sam and myself, my eyes begin to water. I look back at Luna. In the short time she has been here, how was she able to flawlessly capture the feelings Sam and I have for each other? She scribbles on her notepad and holds it in front of her. *I can see it and feel it. You have a lot of love for one another. Love is an emotion; no matter how hard we may try, we can't truly disguise it.*

Lifting my hand and hoping I do it right, I sign, *"Thank you."* The alarm chimes as the front door swings open. "Good morning ladies." Dr. Kendrick steps in, closing the door behind her. At her side is her young son, Josh. "Sorry, I'm running late. Our sitter canceled last minute."

"I don't need a babysitter," her son pouts as he plops down on the chair facing the large living room window. "I can take care of myself."

Dr. Kendrick lets out an exhausted sigh. "Josh," she warns him.

He responds with a sulky expression before digging his phone from the pocket of his shorts. Dr. Kendrick faces me. "You ready?" She gives a tired smile.

"Ready."

She faces Luna and signs something to her, and Luna replies.

As I follow Dr. Kendrick to her office that was once the master bedroom, I ask her, "How long have you known sign language?"

"For six years. There needs to be more people in the world who can communicate with those who are hearing impaired. Everyone deserves to have someone they can talk to, and not all of us communicate the same." She closes the door after I step inside the room. Taking a seat on the couch along the wall, I wait for her to set her things on her desk, grab her notebook and walk back, joining me on the opposite end. "So, what do you feel like talking about? Have you experienced any more anxiety since the other day?"

"No. That attack has been the only one so far this week. Something did happen, though." I try to bring myself to share with her.

"Okay. Good? Bad?" she wonders and waits for me to answer.

I close my eyes, remembering Sam's lips on mine.

"From the content look on your face, I'm going to assume that whatever happened was good." I hear the pleasant tone of her voice and open my eyes.

"Sam kissed me." The words burst out of me with excitement.

"And how did that make you feel?"

My fingers touch my lips. "Like fireworks. I wanted him to kiss me repeatedly," I tell her.

"That's good, Sofia. Are you confused about anything?"

Without hesitation, I confess, "Everything with Sam feels right."

Putting her pen down, Dr. Kendrick sets her notepad aside. "Do you feel like you may be ready for a relationship with Sam?"

In so many ways, we kind of already are. With Sam, our connection has always been a little more than just friendship. He is the one who has been waiting for me to feel comfortable enough to take things further. After that kiss, I feel confident in doing just that. "I feel ready," I nod.

"And what about sex? There will come a point in the relationship you both are ready to explore those feelings more. Before that happens, I think you should talk to Sam. Open up to him about your past and what you have been through. Him knowing certain things can help both of you navigate through a situation that may arise from the trauma you've experienced."

Wow. And just like that, my session just got heavy. To be honest, I have thought about all those things. I enjoy Sam's affection, but he has never gone too far with it. But do I worry about something we might explore together will trigger me? I've never thought much about it before now.

"Would having a session with Sam in the room make it easier for you to share some details with him?" Dr. Kendrick asks.

"I don't know," I answer her with honesty.

"Think about it. You don't have to decide anything yet. Just make sure you talk with him before moving your relationship in that direction."

"Okay," I sigh.

Getting up from the couch, Dr. Kendrick waits for me to stand then wraps her arms around me. "I'm proud of you, Sofia. Be proud of yourself too."

7

SAM

I can't fucking sleep. I can't sleep because the only thing my brain can think about is Sofia. I should have known all it would take was one taste. One taste and I'd be ruined. If I thought I was addicted to Sofia before, I was dead wrong. Closing my eyes, I think about her pouty lips and the way they tasted. The memory causes my dick to stir. Just then, my alarm goes off. Rolling over, I swipe my cell from the bedside table, silencing it. It's 5:00 am, and the guys will be rolling in soon. Just like they do in the evenings after work, they like to meet up here at the clubhouse before the start of the workday to have coffee and shoot the shit. That means my ass needs to be up and have coffee made by the time they walk through the clubhouse doors. Ignoring my raging hard-on, I climb out of bed and make my way to the bathroom. Once I've taken care of business, I snag a pair of jeans from the dresser along with a t-shirt and get dressed. Leaving my room, I walk down the hall and into the kitchen while enjoying the silence surrounding me. I like this time of morning before the other guys roll out of bed and before the other men show up.

When I sit down at the table with my first cup of coffee, a

sleepy-eyed Ember saunters into the kitchen. "Good morning, Sam."

"Mornin', sweetheart."

Ember and Raine are the two club girls that live here at the clubhouse. Both girls are sweet, respectful, and loyal as hell, especially to the old ladies. I heard stories about a couple of club girls that came before them. The old ladies like Ember and Raine. Most of that is due to the fact they stay away from the men who are taken. It seems Ember and Raine have their own little code they live by. I often wonder what leads a woman down the path of becoming a club girl, but I at no time have ever passed judgment. Who anyone takes to their bed is their business. Just because someone enjoys sex, doesn't make them a bad person. Although I have noticed Ember has had only one man warming her bed lately. She and Blake seemed to be exclusive these days. Only neither one of them has acknowledged it publicly. That's their business, though, and as Jake said, a man's business is his own.

Several minutes later, Jake is the first to make an appearance. Not long after he walks through the door, the rest of the men begin to trickle in. Each man goes about fixing their coffee before taking a seat at the table. It's the same routine every morning yet somehow today feels different. The difference is, I am the focus of their attention. Logan is the first to speak. "You and Sofia?"

Setting my cup down, I keep eye contact with him. "Me and Sofia."

Logan continues. "I think I can speak for my brothers when I say we saw this shit was going to come to a head sooner or later. I'm also going to say I respect the hell out of how you've been handling her. You know I'm not telling you what went down with her because it's not mine or anyone else's place. You've been lettin' your instincts guide you the past couple of years, and so far, they have been spot on. With that being said, I don't think any of us need to tell you how much that girl means to the club." Logan leaves his sentence hanging. Something I learned a long time ago about these men is when it comes to the women in their lives; they love hard. They bend over backward to give them hearts and flowers. But don't mistake their actions toward their women as a weakness. Because with that comes the intensity of their loyalty. The Kings have killed to prove their loyalty. They will go through any means necessary to protect the club and their families.

"You have nothing to worry about," I say with certainty. The men study me for a beat before deciding they trust the sincerity of my words. Standing from his seat, Jake raps his knuckles on the table. "Alright, brothers, let's get our asses to work." With that, we follow Jake out of the kitchen. We don't make it two steps into the main room before the door to the clubhouse crashes open, splintering from its hinges. "ATF! Down on the ground!" is shouted, followed by at least a dozen men barging into the clubhouse. Decked out in full ATF gear and weapons drawn, several agents force us down to the ground while several others rush past us down the hall toward the back of the clubhouse. "Motherfucker," Blake seethes as two agents return with a visibly shaken Ember and Raine, then forces them to join us on the floor. "Keep cool," Jake grinds out the same time someone shouts, "Search them!"

One by one, the men are searched, turning up what we all knew the agents would find. Guns. Jake, Logan, Reid, Quinn, Blake, Austin, and Grey are all carrying. "What do we have here?" one of the agents boasts. "You want to tell me where the rest of the guns are?"

"Don't know what the fuck you're talkin' about," Jake replies with venom in his voice.

"Oh, I think you do. I received an anonymous tip that you boys were back to your old habits."

"You can take your tip and shove it up your ass. My men and I got nothin' to say."

"Have it your way." The agent glares at Jake then addresses his fellow agents. "Take them in. Make the call to local. Tell them we'll be needing the use of their station."

Not wasting time, cuffs are slapped on our wrists before we are ushered out of the clubhouse and into the back of a van marked ATF. Once loaded and the door slammed shut, Jake speaks. "Nobody says shit once we get down to the station. Not a goddamn word. I saw they didn't bring Ember and Raine, so I know the girls will get in touch with Bennett," he orders.

"What the hell. Who the fuck do you think sent in a bogus fuckin' tip, Prez?" This coming from Quinn.

Closing my eyes, I shake my head then chance a glance at Jake. No surprise, I see his stare already aimed at me. He knows. This whole shit show is because of me. "You get those thoughts out of your head, son. This isn't on you."

"Do one of you want to explain to the rest of us what the hell is going on?" Logan asks. "Do you two know who the fuck came after the club?"

I go to open my mouth only to have Jake cut me off. "No. We're not doin' this shit here. This is club business, and it will be handled in church. Right now, we focus on the problem at hand."

The remainder of the ride to the police station is done in silence. The energy in the van is so thick it can be cut with a knife, and the vibes coming off Gabriel are damn near suffocating. He's got that wild look in his eyes. "Rein that shit in, Gabriel," Jake warns just before the van comes to a stop, and the back doors are pulled open. "Let's go. Get your asses out," the asshole agent who has a hard-on for the club orders. When we're led into the station, we are taken to a holding cell. Sheriff Harrison gives Jake a subtle nod as he picks up the phone on the reception desk. The club has a solid relationship with our local PD. Our red-faced sheriff looks like he's not too keen on ATF coming into his town and his station doling out orders.

"Tell me what you know about The Kings?" a man who has identified himself as Agent Stuckey when he brought me into an interrogation room asks. He's also the same man who appears to be leading the operation. At this point, the brothers have been separated and placed into separate rooms for questioning. "I know you haven't been around the club long. Now is the time to get out from under them, leave before they ruin your life. These men are not good people. Each one of them has a rap sheet a mile long," Agent Stuckey informs. I stay silent with my arms crossed over my chest as he looks at me, waiting for my answer. I have none. "Look, you're young. You have your whole life ahead of you. You tell me what you know about the club, and I'll make sure you get out of this ordeal unscathed. You probably have some family somewhere who wants you to come home, right?" And there it is. That little remark is all the confirmation I need to confirm this is my father's handy work.

Stretching my legs out in front of me, I lean back in the metal chair I'm sitting on. "I got nothin' to say. You can report back to William McGregor; his tactics won't work on the club or me." I see the look of recognition pass over Agent Stuckey's face just before the door opens, and a fellow agent sticks his head in. "They've lawyered up." When I step out of the holding room, I make my way to the front of the station with the other guys. Standing with them is River. River is a lawyer who happens to be a friend of Reid's woman Mila. He became a friend to the club not long ago when he helped Reid and Mila with some personal shit. "As you can see, you held my clients here under false pretenses. You found nothing when you raided their club, and the weapons you found on their person are legally registered," River informs, producing paperwork.

"So, in other words," Jake grunts, standing in a room full of ATF agents, "ya ain't got shit on us."

Twenty minutes later, we're rolling up to the compound.

Myself, along with Jake, Logan, Reid, and Quinn, hitch a ride with River, while Gabriel, Blake, Austin, and Grey follow behind in Bennett's truck. We file out of the vehicles making our way up to the clubhouse and stop short when Jake halts us from going inside. "You all know word travels fast around here, so you also know our women are inside worried sick. Tend to your old ladies first, then we have church in thirty." Jake looks at me. "Sam, prospects don't normally sit in on church, but today is different. I expect your ass to be in there with the rest of the brothers."

"Yes, sir."

Satisfied with my response, Jake turns and is the first to step inside the clubhouse. Everyone else follows behind. Jake was right. The women are here, and they look visibly shaken. I scan the room, looking for one person. Sofia jumps from her place next to Lisa. Sprinting across the room, she makes a mad dash straight into my arms. Wrapping her arms around me, I pick her up and bury my face in her neck while breathing in her sweet scent. Without a moment's hesitation and with her still in my arms, I carry Sofia to my room. Kicking the door shut with my foot, I sit on the bed with my girl on my lap, her body trembling. "Shh, Firefly." I rub lazy circles on her back.

Finally, she looks at me, her eyes wet. "When I heard what happened, it scared me. I thought something was going to happen to you, to the guys. All we knew was the club had been raided, and you were taken into custody. Then when I got to the clubhouse, it was a mess. The door was busted; there was broken glass everywhere. The rooms were riffled through."

Cupping her face, I say, "I'm fine, the guys are fine. You have nothing to worry about, baby. I promise." Sofia nods, and I wipe away her tears with my thumb. Leaning in, I press my lips against hers, once, twice, then kiss each eyelid. Fisting the front of my shirt, she leans in closer seeking more of my touch. I continue to pepper kisses along her cheek and down her jaw until I connect with her mouth once again. This time, I swipe my tongue across the seam of her lips, and she opens for me. Taking the offered invitation, I take Sofia's mouth completely. I growl when her tongue swirls around mine, taking what it wants, tasting me, and me tasting her. After several moments, I break away—Sofia whimpers at the loss of our connection. I smile and take that as a good sign. I lean my forehead against hers. "I'm going to take everything you're willing to give me, and because I'm a selfish man, I'm going to take everything you're scared to give me because deep down, I know that's what you want."

"Only you," she breathes. "It can only ever be you."

I kiss her forehead. "Looks like we're on the same page."

Running her fingers through my hair, she nods.

"I have to go meet the guys for church. You want to wait in here or go out there with the women?"

"I'll go out there. I want to help clean the place up."

"Alright, baby. Come on." I stand, setting her on her feet. "When I'm done, I'll come to find you."

Nearly an hour later, the sound of the gavel crashing down on the table echoes off the walls in the room where Jake just called church. Lighting a cigarette, he takes a long drag. "First things first. We owe River for comin' down to the station and savin' our asses. We all know good and well, not one of us has a registered piece. I don't know how he did it, but he was able to pull some paperwork out of his ass and squash the only thing ATF could hold us on. Though I suspect ATF doesn't give two shits about what they found on us. They were lookin' for something bigger or nothin' at all."

"What you talkin' about, Prez?" Logan asks.

Cutting his eyes over to me, Jake snubs out his cigarette. His eyeballing me gains everyone's attention. Deciding to man up, I bite the bullet and lay my shit on the table. "I'm pretty sure ATF showin' up is my father sending a warning."

"What the fuck. Your pops a Fed or something?" this coming from Gabriel, though it sounds like a question and not an accusation. For which I am relieved. With every eye in the room trained on me, waiting for an answer, I suck in a deep breath and give them one. "My dad is not the Fed. He is a lawyer. A very well-known lawyer. He's also currently running for Governor of Texas. Needless to say, he has connections as well as a long reach."

"So, what? Your old man is pissed you've taken up with an MC and has decided to stir up shit?" Quinn cuts in.

I shake my head. "It's more than that. I didn't fall in line with his plans for me, which was going to law school and being his puppet. Now he wants me to come home because he's decided to add politics to his resume. He needs to put on a show for the citizens of Texas. To do that, he wants to give them what they want. My dad needs to put on a show, the show of being a well-rounded family man with me at his side during the campaign."

"That's fucked up," Logan voices. "It's also a lot of trouble to go through just to get you to come home."

"It is. But for my father, it's more about power. It's not that he can't run a successful campaign without me; it's because I told him no. William McGregor does not take no for an answer, and he does not back down. He hates that I'm not heeding his demands. I am his only child. Without me, there is no one to pass the family legacy down to. Everything he and my grandfather has built stops with him."

"Jesus Christ," Grey mutters. "That's a fuck load of pressure to put on your kid."

I shrug. "I guess so. But I've always known I wouldn't be following in my dad's footsteps."

The room is silent for several beats while the guys chew on the new-found information I just delivered. It's Gabriel who speaks first. "What's the plan, Prez?"

Jake grins. "You know, New Orleans is not that far from Dallas.

I was thinkin' our boys down south could pay Sam's dad a little visit; give him a taste of his own medicine." Jake turns to me. "As I told you before, Son, no motherfucker is going to dictate how I run my club. I'd bet my left nut William McGregor is bankin' on me thinkin' you aren't worth the trouble and releasing you from the club. The Kings back down to no one. If your dad thinks sending ATF to Polson is going to make me, you or my brother's cave to his threats...he is in for one hell of a wake-up call. Now I want you to get with Reid, and you two are going to get me as much information on this motherfucker as you can."

I return a shit-eating grin of my own. "Yes, sir."

"I'm going to put in a call to Riggs; see if he and the boys are up for a party." With nothing left to be said, Jake slams the gavel ending church.

8

SOFIA

As I'm leaving for work, I spot an old pickup truck I'd never seen before sitting across the street in my side mirror as I back out of the garage. My attention stays fixed on the person sitting behind the wheel while the garage door closes. From the build of the person's body, I would say it's a man. He's wearing a black shirt, trucker's hat, and dark aviator glasses, which mask most of his facial features. Before I fully back out of the driveway, the truck drives off. Maybe he happens to be a family member or a friend of the older couple who lives across the street. With that, I quickly dismiss my initial worries and forget about the guy altogether.

Eager to meet up with Amy for a little retail therapy, I head toward her house. Having an average day is a welcome distraction since the raid on the clubhouse happened two days ago. I'm not aware of all the details surrounding the club's arrest either, but knowing River, an attorney friend of Mila's, was able to help out with the charges against them has helped ease my mind a bit. I was told everything would be okay and for me not to worry about anything. But I do worry. They are my family and Jake is like a dad to all of us. Not to mention, he has two kids of his own and a wife at home. The chaos also put a damper on The Kings' women and I participating in the 5k charity run. I'm no athlete, but I was willing to give it my all from start to finish because the cause is near and dear to my heart. However, Reid lifted my spirits when he suggested us women organize our own charity event for New Hope House in the Fall. In the end, all of the ladies thought it was a fantastic idea.

When I pull up in front of Amy's house, she's sitting on her front porch waiting for me. Rushing down the steps, she makes her way to my car and climbs inside. "I can't wait to enjoy a little pool time. But first bikini shopping." Amy reaches over, turning the volume on the radio up. "So, I heard Sam was in a fight?" she inquires, slipping her sunglasses on.

The fight.

It seems like the entire town is talking about it. "It was nothing. Some drunk guy was looking for a fight," I shrug my shoulders.

"I heard Sam beat the shit out of the asshole," Amy remarks. I fall silent, thinking back to the incident. Out of everything that happened that day, the fight was the one event I'd rather not focus on. I think about our first kiss then all the kisses we have shared since and my cheeks begin to ache from the smile on my face.

"Okay. Spill. There's something you're not telling me. The smile on your face says there is far more to that day's events you haven't shared with me." Amy fixates her eyes on me as she folds her arms across her chest.

"What?"

"Sof, I'm your best friend. I know when you're keeping something from me."

"Sam kissed me," I say, trying to hide the giddiness in my voice.

"Shut up! You guys kissed? Oh my god, Sof. I'm so excited for you. Sam is a great guy. That explains the drunk love look you have on your face."

I can't argue with that.

Pulling into a parking spot in front of the department store, Amy and I frequent any chance we get; the two of us grab our bags, sling them across our bodies and make our way inside. A bell dings over our heads the moment we pull open the door. A young woman from California owns Gypsy Soul Boutique. She opened her store here almost a year ago. I love everything about this store. I haven't seen a thing in here I don't like.

"Sofia and Amy." Clara looks up from the mannequin she is dressing. "I was wondering when you two would be stopping by."

"Yesterday was payday, and my money is burning a hole in my pocket. We need some new bathing suits." Amy spins the display of sunglasses.

"Well, I just got a shipment in yesterday from my best friend in L.A. I haven't unpacked anything yet, but I'll be more than happy to dig a few styles out from the back," Clara mentions as she wraps a brown leather belt around the mannequin cinching the loose-fitting white chiffon dress at the waist.

After spending an hour trying on bathing suits and a few other items, Amy and I head out to Bella and Logan's place.

"Do you think Logan would mind if Ben comes by and hangs with us?" Amy asks as I drive down the road leading to the house.

"I don't see why not." Rolling my car to a stop, I spot Logan under the hood of Bella's car. "He's right there. Why don't we ask him?" Tossing my keys in my purse, we exit the car and grab our shopping haul from the backseat.

"How's it going, baby girl?" Logan wipes his hands on a blue shop rag, as he strolls up to us. Bending, he hugs me and kisses the top of my head. He smells like grease and gasoline. "Need a hand carrying anything?"

"Nope. This is it." I motion toward my friend Amy. "Amy wants to know if Ben can hang out with us?" Amy stands there unmoving as she stares at a shirtless Logan. I nudge her ribs with my elbow to make sure she's still breathing and giggle when she manages to blink. "She seems to be hypnotized by your man muscles." I smile. My teasing provokes Amy enough to finally speak.

"It's not my fault the men in your family are hot." Amy's eyes widen. "Did I just say that out loud?" Her face turns a bright shade of red, and I try not to laugh. Logan doesn't hide his amusement.

"Ben is more than welcome to hang out for a bit," he chuckles, walking back to the front of Bella's car. "Tell my woman I could use a cold beer!" he yells as Amy, and I walk through the open garage to the door.

"I can't believe I said that," Amy says, embarrassed.

"You're just lucky it was Logan you said it to and not one of the other guys like Quinn."

Opening the door, we enter the laundry room. Appearing in the kitchen, we find Bella sitting at the table feeding the kids some macaroni and cheese for lunch.

"Hey, Sof. Hey Amy. It looks like you girls had a successful shopping trip," she says, noticing the bags in our hands. "You two hungry? I have leftovers in the refrigerator."

"I think we are going to head upstairs and change into our bathing suits," I tell her.

"Okay. I'll join you outside as soon as I finish feeding the kiddos, and lay them down for their naps." Bella pets their dog, Bear, on the top of his head as he waits patiently for another macaroni noodle to hit the floor.

Amy follows me up the stairs to my old room. The bags get dumped on my bed, and we start sifting through our things. I hold the gold-colored two piece out in front of me.

"You should wear that one. It's my favorite. The color matches your eyes and looks amazing with your skin tone," she boasts. When I tried it on at the store, I fell in love with the way the light catches the little metallic threads sewn into the fabric.

"Is Sam going to hang out too?" Amy asks as she types away on her phone. Most likely texting Ben.

Walking to the bathroom, I begin peeling my clothes off and pulling on my swimsuit. "I told him last night we were hanging out by the pool today. He said he would try and swing by; that it all depended on what the club has him doing."

"What does prospecting involve?" she asks. Brushing my hair, I answer her. "I'm not entirely sure. All I know is if one of the men tells him to do something, Sam does it; no questions asked. The guys don't talk about a lot of club stuff, and Sam doesn't either."

"Wow. It takes a lot of trust to be with an MC guy. I don't know if I could handle all the secrecy," Amy admits. She's right. Since being a part of the family, there are a lot of things the women are not privy to, but I've come to realize part of it is because they are protecting us. The men are very good at keeping us safe, and a lot of that has to do with keeping club business amongst themselves. Their brotherhood is one of the tightest bonds I have ever seen.

Finished with braiding my long hair, I stand in front of the mirror, admiring the sunburst of color against my skin before stepping out of the bathroom.

Amy gasps. "I'm so jealous right now. Your body is banging, Sof." I look down at myself. She says that to me all the time, but I don't look at myself that way. Not that I don't think I'm pretty. I'm just—me. "Sam is going to die when he sees it on you."

"Ben on his way?" I ask. Slipping on a pair of flip flops, I grab us a couple of towels from the cabinet in the bathroom.

"He should be here in an hour." Grabbing our phones and earbuds off the bed, Amy and I head downstairs.

"Still hard to believe Bella is not much older than you and is a mom. I'm not sure if I'll ever be ready for kids." Her comment makes me ponder the same question. Do I want to have kids someday? It's not a question I've ever really asked myself before. Sliding the patio door open, Amy and I step outside into the warm sunny Montana afternoon. Spreading our towels over the lounge chairs, we stretch out on them. Ready to soak up some sun, I put my earbuds in, and pull up my playlist. After rubbing on some sunscreen, I lean back, close my eyes, and get lost in the music.

A few songs later Ben arrives and he and Amy jump in the pool. Flipping on my stomach, I turn my music down low, and soak up some more sun. As the song *Crazy Love* begins to play, a pair of hands slide over my shoulders and down my spine, causing my skin to prickle under the familiar touch. I don't have to look to know whose hands are on me. My body recognizes his touch. So, I lay there and enjoy Sam's hands on my skin. I hear him pick up the sunscreen bottle then hear the top click as he pops it open then close. Holding my breath, I wait for him to touch me again. His large hands massage the lotion into my skin as he slowly works his way down my back. There's a slight pause before I feel his hands on me again, his palms tortuously skimming my calves, inching higher until he reaches the back of my thighs. My body is on fire. Fingertips graze the bottom of my butt cheeks, creating an explosion of need to course through my veins. I suck in a breath, but I don't dare move. I then feel the earbuds being pulled from my ears, only to be replaced with Sam's hot breath that smells like cinnamon.

"Hey, Firefly." I feel his lips smile against my cheek as he kisses me.

I open my eyes to find him now squatting beside me. His pupils dilate as he drinks in my attire, and notice his heart pulsing through the vein in his neck. Sam wants me as much as I want him. I smile. Raising the upper half of my body, I prop myself up on my forearms. "You gonna kiss me?" I ask him, wanting to feel his lips on mine.

"Absofuckinglutley." Leaning forward, he lifts my chin, pressing his lips against mine.

"I'm happy you're here," I whisper when he pulls away. Sitting on the ground beside my chair, Sam talks with me for a few minutes before Bella appears wearing her bathing suit and holding an envelope in her hand.

"Sof, this letter just came in the mail for you." She walks up to us. Turning over, I sit on the edge of the lounger, and she hands the envelope to me.

"Department of Immigration?" I stare at it a moment. "What could this be about?" My heart pounds with worry. My paperwork and U.S. status are in order. *Right?*

Tearing open the end of the envelope, I pull the letter out and unfold it. Reading it, my heart lodges in my throat. "This says due to incomplete records, my status here in the United States is under review. Investigative actions are being taken. Does this mean I could be at risk of deportation back to Mexico?" I look at Sam than at Bella. "Can they do that?"

Sam rubs my thigh to comfort me.

"Sofia, I don't know, but I'm damn sure about to find out," Bella says in a protective tone.

Logan appears at Bella's side. "What's going on?" he asks. I hand him the letter to read for himself. My eyes fall on Sam. Sucking in a breath of air, I hold in my emotions. "The fuck?" The tone of Logan's voice catches Ben and Amy's attention, and they wade to the side of the pool.

"Sof, are you okay?" Amy questions, and I give her a weak smile.

Logan kisses Bella on the forehead. "I need to make a few calls."

I'm well aware of all the hoops The Kings went through to make sure I stayed in the U.S. But what if something wasn't filed correctly? The smallest of details can slip through the cracks, giving the government reason to act. It may not have been my choice when my family brought me here, but this is my home. It's the only place I want to be. The only place I know I am safe.

"Hey," Sam grabs my attention. "Baby, look at me." Lifting my chin, he brings my eyes level with his. "Trust the club to take care of everything."

Tears threaten to spill, but I hold them back and focus on Sam's handsome face through watery eyes. "I can't go back." Fear settles in my stomach, and the space around me starts to feel like it's closing in on me.

"Sam, help Sofia inside." I barely hear what Bella is saying through the roaring sound in my ears. I feel my body go weightless as Sam picks me up, cradles me in his arms and carries me inside. Not letting go, he walks into the living room and sits on the sofa.

"Is she okay?" I hear Ben ask with worry.

"She's having a panic attack, but she'll be fine soon. Maybe you guys should go for the day. She'll be tired once it passes," Bella explains to Amy and Ben in a calming manner. I'm too far into my attack to protest or feel embarrassed that my best friend and her boyfriend are witnessing this.

"Could you please have her call me when she feels better?" Amy says, her voice full of concern.

"I'll tell her," Bella assures.

"Listen to my voice, baby. Concentrate on your breathing," Sam tries to coach me through it. Focusing on the rise and fall of his chest as he holds me tight, I begin to calm down.

After what feels like forever, I'm able to focus. "I'm feeling better," I tell him. Sam slides me from his lap. "Could I get something to drink?" I ask. Bella and I have been through this before, so it's no surprise she already has a bottle of water in her hand.

"Would you like to go upstairs, maybe lay down for a little while?" she asks as I down half the bottle.

I shake my head. "No. If I do that, I will want to stay, and I need to get back to the house. The other ladies and I are doing pizza and Netflix tonight. It's important to me that I spend time with everyone and get to know them."

Bella doesn't try to convince me otherwise. She knows how important my independence is to me. The look on Sam's face clearly says he thinks otherwise. "At least let me take you home," he offers.

"On your bike?"

"You up for it? I can drive your car and get Reid to pick me up from your place."

An image of him driving my small sun yellow car through town causes me to giggle. "I'm up for it."

After Bella fixes Sam and me a light lunch, I decide it's time to go home. Pausing at the front door, Bella and I hug. "Call me if you need anything and try not to worry. This family—your family will move mountains to make sure nothing happens to you," she tells me before letting go.

"Thanks, Bella."

"Momma!" I hear little Jake call from the playroom. Bella smiles. "I'll see you later, Sof."

Climbing down the steps, Sam takes my hand and leads us in the direction of his motorcycle. We pause by his bike, and I wait for him to slip a helmet over my head. Looking over my shoulder, I wave at Bella, who's still standing at the front door.

The ride on the back of Sam's bike was the therapy I needed after receiving that letter. Cruising down the road with the wind in my hair and the sun on my face was all it took to wash away my worries for now. Reaching back, Sam's hand wraps around my calf. Leaning against his back, I wrap my arms around his torso, running my hands across his abs and ride like that the entire way home.

Pulling up to the house, Sam parks his bike in the driveway. After helping me remove the helmet, I climb off the back of his motorcycle. Tucking me into his side, he walks me to the front door. "I'll pick you up tomorrow and take you back to Bella's to get your car." We step onto the porch, and he faces me.

"Okay." I wait before unlocking the door for him to kiss me.

"Come here," he rasps. Tugging on the waistband of my shorts, he pulls me closer. "Give me your lips." Waiting for me to take the lead, Sam looks down at me. His hand takes hold of my hips. Placing my palms on his shoulder, I raise on my tiptoes. With the movement, my cropped shirt rises. Sam's hands go from my hips to the shallow sides of my waist before skimming his palms higher up my ribcage as my lips descend upon his. Fueled by desire, he deepens the kiss. Parting my lips, our tongues tangle together setting me on fire. We've shared several kisses since our first, but this one feels different. Once we break free, I feel lightheaded.

"I gotta go, baby."

Nodding, I unlock the door and walk inside the house, knowing he won't leave until I have shut and locked the door behind me. Peeking through the window, I watch Sam mount his bike. Bringing my fingertips to my lips, I think about the kiss we'll share tomorrow as I watch him drive away.

THE REST of the evening flies by as me and the women binge watch Netflix while devouring two large pizzas. In food comas, we call it a night. A few hours later, I wake, needing to go to the bathroom. When I've finished, I shuffle down the hall toward the kitchen to get myself a glass of water. Crossing the living room, I catch what appears to be a shadow pass by the window outside, and I freeze. Thinking my sleepy eyes must be playing tricks on me, I rub them and continue to stare at the window. After a few seconds of watching the window and seeing nothing, I shrug my shoulders and proceed to the kitchen. Downing a glass of water, I head back to bed. However, curiosity and paranoia get the better of me, and I walk over to the window, slightly part the blinds and peer outside.

The porch is well lit, and I see nothing out of the norm. It's not until I scan the street do I notice the same truck I saw before, parked across the street. I squint my eyes, but I'm not able to make out much since it's dark outside. Movement from the cab of the truck makes the hairs on my neck stand. The red glow from the end of a cigarette illuminates the bottom half of the person's face. My heart pounds hard against my chest, and everything in me says I should call Sam. Rushing to my room, I snatch my phone from the nightstand and run back into the living room. I look down at my phone screen. "Crap, it's 2:00 am," I whisper. Pulling up Sam's number, I swipe the screen.

"Sofia?"

"Sam," I speak low, not wanting to wake the others. "There's a truck parked across the street. I saw the same truck this morning." I hear rustling on the other end of the line.

"Babe, can you see someone in this truck?"

"Yes."

"Okay. Listen, I'm further away, so I'm going to put you on hold and call Reid. He can get there quicker. Stay on the phone."

I nod even though he can't see it. "Okay." Not even a full minute passes before Sam's voice breaks the silence.

"Baby?"

"I'm still here," I tell him.

"Reid is on his way. I'll be there as soon as I can," he assures me. "I've got you on Bluetooth, so stay on the line."

Standing by the window, I continue to watch the truck. I hear the roar of Sam's engine the moment he fires up his bike. "How are you doing, beautiful?"

"He's still there."

"Are the other women with you?"

"No. They're still asleep." I glance over my shoulder in the dark hallway. Turning my attention back to the window, I catch the truck pulling away with the headlights off. "Sam, the truck is leaving." I watch as far as my eyes can see until the truck is no longer in sight. Maybe ten minutes pass before the distinct rumble of a Harley gets louder the closer it gets to my house.

"Are you down the road?" I see a headlight glowing in the distance as I look out the window.

"No, baby. That should be Reid. I'm still ten minutes out."

I watch as Reid drives his bike past the house then doubles back before pulling into the driveway and directly in front of the steps leading to the porch.

"Reid will probably check the perimeter first. He'll let himself in when he's done," Sam explains before I try opening the door.

When Reid finishes, he steps onto the porch and punches in the security code for my house into his phone. He finds me standing by the window as soon as he steps inside.

"Sam, Reid is inside now; I'm going to let you go."

"I'll see you soon," he assures, then the call ends.

"I'm sorry, Reid."

"Nothing to apologize for, Sweetheart. Sam said you saw the same truck this morning too?"

I nod. "He drove away, leaving his lights off before you got here. But before all that, when I first came out to get a drink of water, I could have sworn I saw a shadow outside this window." I point behind him.

"I'm going to go into Dr. Kendrick's office and access the security feed. I think it may be a good idea to wake the women before the guys arrive. We don't need anyone freaking out."

I should have known all the men would be called in. He's right. I don't think Emma will be too upset, but Luna is a different story. With Reid in the office, I first knock on Emma's door. Reaching over, she turns on the lamp sitting on her nightstand. After explaining what's happened and that the guys will be arriving soon, I ask her to go with me to Luna's room. Turning the knob, we find her room lightly lit from the TV being left on. Her eyes pop open the moment I touch her arm. Looking confused, she sits up and leans against the headboard. She looks past my shoulder to Emma, who is standing by the door. Turning her lamp on, I sit down on the edge of the bed and explain to her why we woke her up. I do my best to assure her The Kings are good men, and she has no reason to be afraid. "You feeling okay?" I ask once I've finished explaining the situation.

Grabbing her notepad, she responds. *I'm okay. I trust you.*

I leave Emma with Luna and walk back out to the living room. When I reach the end of the hallway, I peek inside Dr. Kendrick's office, where I see Sam has arrived along with Grey and Jake. They are huddled together watching the computer screen alongside Reid. I can't hear what they are saying, but the looks on their faces suggest concern. I watch as Jake reaches into his cut pulling out a pistol. He hands it to Sam. Before I'm caught watching, I walk into the office making my presence known. Jake sees me first, which causes Sam to turn. Tucking the gun away, he strides toward me.

"Hey baby." He pulls me in for a hug.

"Sam is staying here tonight," Jake announces, stepping out of the office. "On the couch," he adds, making eye contact with Sam.

Knowing they would tell me more if necessary, I don't ask any questions. "I'll go get you some sheets and a pillow." Walking down the hall, I dig around in the linen closet, grabbing Sam a pillow, and two sheets. The rest of the men are gone, and Sam is resetting the alarm when I return. I get to work fixing the couch for him so he can get some sleep. Taking a chance, I ask him, "Do they know who the guy was? Should we be worried?"

Sam helps by slipping the pillowcase over the pillow. "The club is looking into it."

I sigh, knowing he won't divulge more. "There's a good-sized throw on the back of that chair," I point across the room, "if you need more than this sheet."

Stepping closer, Sam plants a soft kiss on my lips. "Let the other women know I'm here." He kisses my forehead. "Get some rest. I'm not going anywhere."

A yawn escapes me. "I can do that."

Sam lowers himself to the sofa and pulls his boots off his feet. I look over my shoulder before entering the hallway. "Goodnight, Sam."

"Goodnight, Firefly."

9

SAM

S tretching the kinks out of my sore back, I stand from the sofa, grab my pistol from the coffee table, reach behind me, and slide it into the waistband of my jeans. Last night when Sofia called saying someone was watching the house, I didn't waste any time jumping on my bike and hauling ass to her house when I heard the fear in her voice. The sound of a sharp intake of breath steals my attention. I turn to see Sofia standing just inside the living room entrance, holding two coffee mugs. I watch as she rakes her eyes up and down my bare torso. "Mornin', baby."

Her eyes dart up to mine as a pretty blush stains her cheeks. "Good morning," she squeaks. "I, ah, made you some coffee," she stammers, holding up the cup.

Plucking my shirt up off the floor, I stride up to Sofia, take the offered coffee and kiss the corner of her mouth. "Thanks, baby. I'll be right back. I'm going to hit the head."

"Okay. I put a spare toothbrush on the sink for you."

I wink. "Thanks."

Once I've finished my business, I find Sofia in the kitchen frying bacon and scrambled eggs. "You hungry?"

"Yeah. I could eat."

Loading our plates, she piles mine with triple the amount she fixes herself then joins me at the table where we eat in silence. I see her emotions playing out on her face and know she's thinking about last night. "Look at me, baby," I demand. She stops eating and gives me her full attention. "It's going to be okay. I won't let anything happen to you."

"It's not just me I'm worried about. I want the women staying here to feel safe too. They come here to escape danger, Sam."

"The club won't let anything happen to them either, Sofia. You know that, don't you?"

She nods. "I know. I can't help but worry."

A knock on the door interrupts our conversation. Standing from the table, I make my way to the front door. Looking through the blinds, I notice Grey standing on the porch. Opening the door, I let him in. "Hey, man. Prez sent me. He wants you at the clubhouse. I'll stay here with the girls."

Nodding, I walk over and grab my cut lying on the back of the sofa before making my way to Sofia, who is still sitting at the kitchen table. "I'll be back later, baby," I assure her. "Now, give me your mouth." My demand earns me a smile as she stands, raises on her tiptoes, and gives me what I asked for.

The first thing I notice when I pull up to the clubhouse is Demetri's black SUV. Logan's dad has been out of the country for a couple of weeks, so I'm curious as to why he is here. Demetri and his other son Nikolai share a home here in Polson. The two moved to Montana a few years ago after reconnecting with Logan. Nikolai went into business with The Kings while Demetri shuffles back and forth between Polson and Russia as he runs his empire. The family doesn't air too much of Demetri's business, but from what I have gathered since living here and hanging around The Kings, Volkov's are Mafia.

When I enter the clubhouse, Logan happens to be the only

person I see. He's sitting at the bar talking on his phone when he spots me. Ending his conversation, he jerks his chin. "Come on. The brothers are waitin' on us." I follow behind him as we make our way to the room the club holds church. Entering the room, I'm met by the whole club, including Demetri and Nikolai. It's not unusual for Logan's dad and brother to be involved with club business, so I don't give their presence in church another thought. Once Logan and I have taken our seat, Jake slams the gavel. I'm the first person he addresses.

"How's Sofia doin' this mornin'?"

"She's still a bit shaken up. Whoever that motherfucker was last night has my girl scared out of her mind."

"You all know it goes without sayin' I want Sofia, her house and the women stayin' there to have around the clock protection until we get a handle on who we are dealin' with," Jake orders.

Without hesitation, I speak up. "I want to be the one watchin' my girl."

Leaning back in his chair with his arms crossed over his chest, Jake ponders my request while keeping his steel gaze on mine. I will admit he's pretty damn intimidating right now, but Sofia is mine; therefore, I'm not backing down from what I want. Finally, after several beats, Jake opens his mouth. "You claimin' her, son?" The guys know I have voiced my interest in Sofia, but I know at this moment Jake asking me this question is making what Sofia and I have official.

"Yes, sir. Sofia is mine." The second the words leave my mouth, there is a chorus of "hell, yeahs" filling the room.

Jake slams the gavel once again, bringing the attention of his men back to him. "Sam will stay with Sofia. That means, for now, your only job is to protect her. When she's at work, your ass is outside waitin' on her until she's done. She needs to go anywhere; it's on the back of your bike. Also, you will continue to stay at New Hope House. If at any time you encounter a threat, you call one of the brothers for backup. Are we clear?" he asks me.

"Yes, sir. We're clear."

Next, Jake turns his attention to Reid. "I want you out at Sofia's place, checking on the security equipment. Go ahead with the motion sensors too. I don't like how that son of a bitch was able to get as close as he did. I also want you to sync the security feed at her place to all our phones. If something else like last night happens again, I want all the brothers informed."

"You got it, Prez," Reid nods.

Lighting a cigarette, Jake brings up another piece of information. "Logan informed me yesterday Sofia received a letter in the mail from Immigration Services."

"What the fuck?" Gabriel growls.

"Those fuckers are trying to question her status. I don't even know why the hell she's on their radar." The moment those words leave Jake's mouth, I curse.

"Fuck."

"What ya thinkin', Sam?"

"I can't say for sure, but my gut says Sofia getting that letter has something to do with my dad." I shake my head.

"Speaking of," Quinn jumps in. "What's the status of Riggs and his men, Prez?"

Jake grins. "Let's put a call in now and see what our boys are up to." Using the landline on the table, Jake dials a number then puts the call on speaker. Riggs answers on the second ring.

"Brother."

"What do you got for me, man?"

"McGregor won't be a problem anymore," Riggs states, gaining the room's attention. "Tell Reid to check his email. Kiwi sent a little present." With that, he hangs up.

All eyes turn to Reid as he begins typing away on his laptop. He picks up a remote and turns on the TV in the corner of the room. A second later, a video plays out on the screen, and my father's voice fills the room. "What the hell is going on! Get out of my house before I call the police!" he booms the same time a young woman scurries out of his bed in haste to cover her naked body. When I say young, I mean she barely looks legal.

"You sure you want to be callin' the police?" Riggs taunts. Turning to the girl, he asks, "How old are ya, sweetheart?"

"Hey! What are you doing over there?" my dad asks, looking over Riggs's shoulder, his face turning a nice shade of white. "Turn that camera off!"

"No. I don't think we will. Kiwi, you keep that camera rollin'."

"Look. I'll pay. I have the money. Just take what you want and leave." The crack in my father's voice says he knows he's in deep shit.

"How do you think the citizens of Texas would react knowin' their potential governor likes dippin' his wick in barely legal pussy?" Riggs continues to taunt.

"She's twenty. But still, you can't show that video."

Riggs, without a care in the world, strolls over to a chair in the corner of my dad's bedroom, sits with his legs spread wide, lights a cigarette, and cocks his head to the side. "That's right. It's not your little girlfriend's age that has you shittin' your pants now, is it?" He takes another drag of his cigarette. "You don't want people knowin' you're fuckin' a judge's daughter. You seem to have gotten yourself into a hole you can't dig out of."

"What is it you want?" my father asks Riggs.

"Word is you been fuckin' with my brothers. I'm gonna assume you weren't bankin' on how far of a reach The Kings have. Know this motherfucker; there ain't a place on earth The Kings can't touch." Riggs's voice turns to ice as he stands, drops his cigarette on my dad's bedroom floor, and snubs it out with his boot. "Besides ATF, you got any more surprises for my friends?" Riggs questions, and my dad nods.

"Spit it out. The Kings don't take too kindly to surprises."

I watch my father visibly swallow. But my dad being the asshole he is, throws in one last dig, consequences be damned. "I reported my piece of shit son's girlfriend to immigration. Sam is nothing but a fuck up and a disappointment to his family." The moment the words leave William McGregor's mouth, Riggs advances on him, delivering a mighty blow to the side of his head, knocking him unconscious. The video ends, and the room falls silent.

I had suspected my dad was behind the ATF and Sofia receiving the letter, but it didn't make it any easier to hear coming straight from his mouth. It's a hard pill to swallow, knowing my father hates me enough to hurt innocent people like my girl.

"Son, look at me." Jake breaks through the suffocating silence filling the room, and I bring my attention to him.

"Your old man is wrong. You are not what he says. Ya, hear me? You are a damn fine man. The Kings are your family, and this family is fuckin' proud of who you are." I take Jake's words to heart because they are the only words that matter.

It's late by the time I leave the clubhouse. After we concluded my father would no longer be a problem since The Kings now had enough leverage to ruin his career, I hit the road. Demetri had offered to take care of immigration, stating he knew a guy, and Jake accepted. We can breathe easy, knowing Sofia's status is safe. At least that is one piece of good news I can deliver to her this evening. As for the situation with the guy who was seen snooping around on New Hope House property last night, we have Reid doing what he does best while the club remains vigilant. It's only a matter of time before he shows again.

After I make it to Sofia's, I give Grey a rundown of what transpired during church before he goes back to the clubhouse. As

I walk the perimeter of the house, I get a text from Reid stating all looks good. He must have obtained an alert from the motion sensors and saw it was me out here. Once I make my way inside, I set the alarm, slip my cut off, and hang it on a hook beside the front door. The house is mostly dark aside from a lamp in the living room, and when I glance down the hall, I see Sofia's bedroom light on. Knowing she's probably finishing up some work, I decide to grab a bite to eat. I smile when I stroll into the kitchen and find a covered plate and a small piece of paper lying on top with my name scribbled on it. My girl is always thinking of others. My stomach rumbles when I remove the foil and find fried chicken, mashed potatoes, and green beans.

With my belly full, I plop down on the sofa, lean my head back, and let out a deep sigh. After the shit day I've had, I find being here, being close to Sofia, makes it all better. Feeling a dip in the cushion beside me, I turn my head to see my girl sitting there. "Hey, baby."

"Long day?" she asks.

"You could say that."

"You want to talk about it?"

Sighing, I sit forward, resting my elbows on my knees. "Shit with my dad was taken care of. So was the letter you received."

"The letter...that was your dad?"

"Yeah, baby. I'm sorry. But you have nothing to worry about. The club handled it."

"You have nothing to be sorry for, Sam. You didn't do anything."

"No. But he did it because of me." I shake my head. "My father confirmed that today when he said I was nothin' but a piece of shit disappointment."

"Sam," Sofia whispers.

"You want to know what's fucked up? My dad saying those things don't even bother me anymore. Not like it used to. Not like when I was a kid. What pisses me off is what he did to the club. To you."

"So your dad said that stuff to you when you were a kid?" Her eyes water.

"Don't cry for me, Firefly." I wipe away the tears escaping down her cheek. "Having my mother made up for having a shitty father."

"Will you tell me about her?"

I smile. "My mom was sweet, quiet, and soft-spoken, yet she was fierce. She was a momma bear through and through. I sometimes wondered what it was about my dad that she was drawn to. She told me once my father wasn't always the asshole he is now. My mom and dad met at college. Mom was from a small town in Texas and raised on a farm. My dad is from Dallas. He came from a respected family and followed in my grandfather's footsteps. She said the more successful he became, so did his need for perfection. My dad became obsessed with his image. Mom went from being the wholesome country girl to a polished socialite. But that was just her image on the outside. On the inside, she was still her true self. Caroline Presley never forgot her roots. Dad hated the fact mom would take me to the farm every chance she got. Long weekends, spring break, and even a few weeks during the summer. My grandfather taught me how to tend to the animals, how to ride a four-wheeler, how to hunt. I spent every Christmas with my grandfather out on the farm. The times I spent camping and hunting with him are some of the best memories I have. When I was sixteen, my grandfather passed away and left my mom the house and their land. My grandmother had died two years before that." I stop and take a moment to reflect on that time before I continue. "Six months after my grandfather died, my dad sold the farm. Right out from under my mom." I shake my head. "I don't know how he did it since everything was in her name. All I know is my mom was devastated. The one true piece of her past and who she was, he took from her. When she broke down and confronted him, he lost his cool and hit her."

Sofia gasps. "Oh my god, Sam."

"It wasn't the first time he had hit her, but it was the first time I witnessed it. My mom had been covering black eyes and bruises for as long as I could remember. I never told her I knew. Just like I had never told her my father was doing the same to me. That was until I hit a growth spurt and became bigger than him."

"Sam, why didn't you ever tell her he was hitting you?"

"Because she would have blamed herself."

"Mother and son, both carrying the same burden," Sofia whispers through the tears she's unable to hold back.

"What happened to your mom?"

"When I was seventeen, I had come home late after celebrating with my team after we had won our championship football game. I was worried because my mom hadn't shown up to the game. She never missed a game, and she especially wouldn't have missed the championship. When I pulled up in the driveway of our home, I saw dad's car was gone, which wasn't unusual. I knew he had a woman on the side, and I suspected mom knew too. Anyway, what alarmed me was mom's car parked in the garage. The first thing I thought was she must be sick, so I raced inside and up the stairs to her bedroom. I knocked on her bedroom door, and there was no answer. I opened it and went inside to find it empty. I noticed the bathroom light was on and the door cracked. When I called out her name, I still got nothing. I remember feeling like my heart was going to beat out of my chest because I knew something was wrong." I look at Sofia. She has scooted herself closer to me and is now clutching the hem of my shirt.

"Oh, Sam. No."

"I found her on the bathroom floor. She had taken sleeping pills." I pull in a deep breath. The memory of finding my mother's lifeless body lying on the bathroom floor is a vision that will forever plague me. I don't hate my mom for what she did; I hate she felt so utterly and completely lost that she thought she had no other way out. My father had used her up until she didn't recognize who she was anymore. The only thing I can take away from the soul-crushing experience is knowing she no longer suffers. She is in a place of peace, and I take comfort in that thought. I also take pleasure in knowing I fulfilled the only dream my mom had for me. I got out. I got out and found my purpose.

10

SOFIA

Facing Sam, I reach for his hand and hold it tight in mine. He just shared so much of himself with me, and I wonder if I can be just as brave. "Baby, you okay?" Sam's brows crease with concern. Tears spill from my eyes for him. For his mother. And at that moment, I decide to share my past with him.

Looking down at our joined hands, I take a deep breath. Before I lose my nerve, I start from the beginning. "I grew up poor. No money. Not much in material things but never lacking in love. Drug Cartels controlled everything, and our town was controlled by Los Demonios, an MC known to be on the Cartel's payroll. My father worked many odd end jobs, but never making enough to get us to where he could afford to move us into better housing." Sam gives my hand a reassuring squeeze to keep going. "I went to school. My mom and I walked almost an hour twice a day to get me there, but she was determined I would get an education so that someday I could make a better life for myself." My thoughts drift back in time and images of my parents appear. "Things went from bad to worse just before I turned fourteen. My dad lost his job and couldn't find work unless he went to live hours away or tried to cross the border, but he wasn't willing to leave his family behind because the crime was getting bad in the area. Women and children turning up missing were becoming more of an occurrence, so my father being desperate started working for Los Demonios." I close my eyes, fighting back the storm brewing deep inside.

"I'm right here, baby." Sam encourages me to stay strong.

Opening my eyes, I look at him. "My parents started fighting after that, which was something they never did before. My mother knew Papa wasn't being truthful about the type of work he was doing, and to this day, I still don't know what he did." Lifting my hand, I wipe my tears away. "He stole from them, Sam. Out of desperation, my father stole from Los Demonios, which is the same as stealing from the Cartel themselves. He took the money he was supposed to take back to Los Demonios, and instead took us across the border into the U.S." I hang my head, still angry with my father for being so stupid.

I would have rather lived the rest of my life as we were—poor, but together and alive than for him to have done what he did because he felt he had no other way out. "He didn't tell us this. My mother and I knew nothing of his crime until the day Los Demonios found him." I take a shuddered breath. "They beat him. There was so much blood." The next parts of my story, I know Sam will find hard to listen to, but I can't stop now. I need to keep going. I need to purge my body of all the memories I've kept locked up inside for so long. I lock eyes with Sam. "That was the last night I saw my parents. Los Demonios took me as payment for my father's sins, just before they took his life with a single bullet. I don't know what happened to my mother. I never saw her again." My heart aches at the thought of what those monsters could have done to her.

Sam brushes away the hair stuck to my tear-soaked skin. He

runs his palm up my arm. "You feel okay? If you need to stop, I understand."

I shake my head. "I need to keep going. There are things about me you need to know."

Sam hands me a tissue from the box sitting on the coffee table, and I wipe my nose. "If I stop now, Sam, I might not have the courage to say these words out loud again," I confess. "For two years, I was kept—nothing more than property for them to use as they pleased. Antonio staked claim to me." I drop my head again. "He used me up, Sam. He used me in any manner he pleased." Sucking my lungs full of air, I look up, straight into Sam's blue eyes. The vein throbbing in his neck and the clenching of his jaw lets me know he's fighting to hold back his rage, but he doesn't interrupt me. "In one night, I lost my father, my mother, and my innocence. I lost everything. They ripped my soul to shreds day in and day out."

Suddenly my mouth feels dry, and my heart feels like it's about to burst from my chest as I try to shake the memory of Antonio's cold, menacing hands on my body. I swallow hard past the lump trying to form in my throat. "He shared my body with his friends. They all took turns. For two years, it was a struggle to survive and not give up." I pause, taking another deep breath but keep going, "There were times when I thought about ending it all."

I watch Sam's face fall at my confession. I know it's not something he wants to hear. Knowing what he went through with his mother, I can understand, but this is my truth, and I need him to know there were moments I was weak, so I keep going. "At times, I felt ending my existence would bring me peace. But then I realized I'm stronger than that. I'm stronger than they are. I was not going to let evil triumph."

Every vile moment I lived through over those two years hits me like a freight train. Then I think of the moment I met Bella. She gave me more hope. When she promised not to leave without me,

I believed her. Then The Kings took me in. Gave me a home when I had none. My fist slams against my chest as I proclaim, "I chose to live." I finally break with those last words. My body no longer able to hold all my emotions, I begin to sob harder than I have ever done before.

"Baby," Sam whispers as he wraps me in his strong embrace. His palm strokes my hair. "You are so much stronger than you realize."

The tears rolling down my cheeks lessen, as Sam continues to hold me in his arms. I feel light. Expelling all those memories lifted a weight I have been carrying around for some time. It feels like the tears cleansed my soul. We sit like this for a while until I start to grow tired. My eyes feel heavy, and I yawn.

"You ready for bed?" Sam asks.

"Not yet. Hold me a little longer?"

Shifting his weight, Sam pulls me with him as he settles back against the couch. Naturally, I tuck my body against his side. Reaching behind us, Sam grabs the throw blanket from the back of the couch, draping it across us. Picking up the remote, he turns the TV on, and he holds me.

I wake to the lite sounds of snoring and a lot of body heat. Realizing I'm lying against Sam's chest, I raise a bit to find us stretched out on the couch, the upper half of my body lying on top of his, while the rest of me is trapped between him and the couch. Deciding I should probably go to my room for the night before the other houseguests find us, I start to move. Trying not to wake him, I slowly sit up. Before leaving, I sit there on my knees and watch Sam sleep. I take the time to study his face, watching the way his lips part every time he exhales.

Suddenly, I feel a pair of large hands graze the sides of my knees then slowly make their way up my thighs, leaving a trail of heat in their path. Peeling my eyes off his body, I lift my gaze to his. The intensity of his stare burns through me, causing my body to tingle with a need for him to touch me and put his lips on mine. Only Sam makes me feel this way. And right now, I'm choosing to act on those feelings. My eyes stay locked on his. Leaning forward, I rest my palms on his chest and watch his pupils dilate. It fuels my desire to keep going. I don't know what has come over me, but I let it happen. I let my passion for Sam guide my movements. Dipping my head, I graze my lips across his, allowing my breath to dance across his skin. My lips travel to the side of his neck. When I get to the spot just below his ear, he hisses.

Sam shifts, bringing himself upright against the arm of the couch, pulling my body toward him. I straddle his lap and run my hands across his broad shoulders. In this position, I feel his arousal pressing against my center. Unable to hold back, I kiss him. His hand slips beneath my shirt as his lips travel down the shallow curve of my neck, and his fingertips graze the sides of my breasts.

I need more.

I want so much more.

I want to drown in his touch.

These thoughts keep repeating in my head as the ache grows between my legs. Seeking relief, I grind against him. His hands drop to my ass, gripping me as I rub against him, seeking friction. I need more, but I know Sam. He's taking his time, going slow for me. Pausing only for a moment, I lock eyes with him as I begin to lift the hem of my shirt. My heart pounds faster than I ever thought possible as I expose myself. Casting my shirt to the floor, I watch Sam's face as he drops his eyes to my breasts, drinking me in.

"You're so fucking beautiful," he tells me. The moment his hands palm my breasts, my skin bursts into flames. I throw my head back as he touches me. I never knew it could feel like this. Then I feel his hot breath against my skin as he kisses the valley between my breasts, and my desire intensifies.

"I need more," I beg. His head lifts to look at me. I move against him, my body asking for more. "Please, Sam."

"Babe, are you sure? I can wait. It doesn't have to go any further than this."

I give him a firm nod. "Take me to bed, Sam. I don't want to wait another second." In one smooth motion, Sam stands. Keeping my legs wrapped around his hips, he carries me down the hall.

11

SAM

With my woman in my arms, I carry her into the bedroom and shut the door with my foot, while refusing to take my eyes off hers. Sofia's body trembles slightly as her nerves kick in, but her eyes are bright, and they tell me she is confident with her decision. She has chosen to trust me with not only her heart but her body, a body which she has never given to a man willingly. My girl has never experienced pleasure or what it's like to have someone who loves you worship the gift you've handed them. Instead, she had hers taken from her. So, tonight, my mission is to show Sofia her body will always be safe with me. I will cherish every inch of her skin and give her the pleasure she deserves. Continuing to take things slow, I sit on the edge of the bed with her sitting on my lap and her legs wrapped around my waist. I ignore the way my dick strains against my zipper as I run my hands up her abdomen until I cup her breasts. She grips the back of my neck, tips her head back and lets out a throaty moan when my thumbs brush over her nipples. Taking advantage of her exposed throat, I lean forward and gently bite the space that throbs with every beat of her heart. Next, I snake my arms around her back until my hands grasp her shoulders, urging her to lean back on my forearms. Tilting her back slightly, Sofia arches her back, thrusting her perfect tits forward. Leaning in, I take one in my mouth. The moment my hot tongue swirls around her nipple, she begins to grind her pussy against my jean covered cock. Releasing her nipple with a pop, I move on to the next, giving it equal attention. I could spend hours just on her tits alone. "Sam," Sofia rasps, digging her nails in my forearms.

"You good, baby? You like my mouth on your tits?" I ask, flicking my tongue over her nipple again as she grinds down harder on my cock.

"Yes," she hisses.

"Look at my girl. So fuckin' beautiful. So sexy." I continue to lick and nip at her luscious body. "Your tits taste so damn good. I bet your pussy tastes even better." Sofia shivers at my words, so I continue. "Will you let me have a taste, Firefly? You want me to make you come with my mouth?"

Without hesitation, she answers, "Yes."

Standing, I cup Sofia's ass as she drapes her arms over my shoulders. Before lowering her to the bed, I take her mouth with mine and our tongues battle, eager for each other's taste. I could spend an eternity tasting Sofia, and it wouldn't be near enough time to get my fill. Placing one knee on the bed, I lay her down in front of me. Her tan skin flushed, and her eyes filled with lust. Slowly I begin to undress as I carefully gauge her reaction with each article of clothing I lose. Starting with my shirt, I grip the material, pulling it over my head, tossing it to the floor. Next, I toe off my boots, at the same time I unbutton my jeans and slide the zipper down, exposing my boxer briefs. With hooded eyes, Sofia's tongue darts out, sliding across her bottom lip. Taking that as a good sign, I lose my jeans completely.

"I want to see," she rasps as I stand at the foot of the bed with my very noticeable hard-on tenting my briefs. Giving my woman what she wants, I tug my boxers down and my cock springs free—Sofia's breath hitches. For a split second, I worry about her state; until I see her clutching the sheets while rubbing her legs together, trying to ease the ache between her thighs. Reaching down, I take her ankles in my hands and slowly pull her to the end of the bed until her legs hang off the edge. Dropping to my knees in front of her, I spread her legs. With her silk sleep shorts still on, I bring my face flush against her heated center, and I can smell her arousal. The sweet musky scent of Sofia's pussy has my dick so hard it begins to leak pre-cum. Looking up from between her legs, I meet her gaze. "I'm going to take these shorts off now." Sofia bites her lip and nods as I grab the waistband of her shorts and slide them down over her legs, exposing her light pink panties. Her breathing begins to increase with each kiss I trail up the inside of her thigh until I reach my intended destination. Unable to resist, I tug her panties to the side and take my first taste of her bare, slick pussy. I immediately become addicted, just as I knew I would. The moment my tongue slides through her slit, her hips buck forward. "Oh, god," she moans, and I smile. Losing herself in the moment, Sofia fists the hair on my head, and I welcome the burn to my scalp. My woman is giving in to the pleasure just as I wanted her to. I want her to lose herself in the moment and think of nothing but us and the way I'm making her feel. I want to drown out her darkness and give her an experience that will help heal her soul. "That's it, Firefly. Take what you need and know it's your man giving it to you," I say just before my mouth devours her pussy once again. I lick her from top to bottom before flicking my tongue over her swollen clit. Sofia's legs start to quiver, and I know she's close to coming. I then run my index finger through her folds, getting it wet with her juices before slipping it inside her. The moment I contact her g-spot, she gasps. "Sam."

"Come for me," I demand just before I suck her clit into my mouth. Sofia comes with a strangled cry as her pussy spasms around my finger, and I lap up her essence. I continue to lick and kiss her pussy until the tremors subside, and her body goes lax.

Standing, I dip down and pull Sofia's sated body further up the bed then remove her panties, tossing them to the floor. Clutching the back of my head, she brings my face to hers and kisses me. My cock hangs heavy between our bodies, but I control the urge to take things further. That is until Sofia brings her feet up to the back of my legs and forces me to give her my weight. I groan the moment my dick comes in contact with her still wet pussy. "I want to feel you inside me," she says, breaking our kiss.

"Are you sure? We can stop here? We don't have to go all the way tonight."

Sofia thrusts her hips. "I've never been more sure of anything in my life, Sam. The thing is I thought I'd be scared, but I'm not. I'm never scared with you. Right now, I feel good. You make me feel good. You make me want more."

Planting my forearms on either side of her head, I touch my forehead to hers. "You make me want more too." Sofia's eyes go soft. She knows I'm talking about more than just this moment. Taking her mouth once again, I thrust my hips, and my cock glides through the hot wet folds of her pussy. I continue to thrust back and forth, teasing us both. I watch Sofia's face, gauging her reaction as she lets out a throaty moan each time the head of my cock nudges her clit. "Sam," she breathes, moving her hips meeting mine thrust for thrust.

"Let me get a condom from my wallet, baby," I say as I go to move only to have Sofia wrap her legs tighter around me.

"I'm protected, and I'm clean," she says on a whisper, her eyes a little guarded. I know the last bit of information is what has her looking at me the way she is now. "I want to feel all of you."

"Shh, baby." I soothe peppering kisses along her jaw and down her neck. "I know, Firefly. You're so damn beautiful, so perfect."

Pulling back, I see tears spilling from her eyes. "Say it. Say you're beautiful."

"I'm beautiful."

"Say you're perfect."

She smiles. "I'm perfect."

"Now tell me you're mine," I demand, my eyes burning into hers.

"I'm yours, Sam."

With our heated gaze on one another, I lift Sofia's leg further up my hip, opening her up to me. Pulling back, I nudge her opening with the head of my cock. My eyes continue to bore into hers as I slowly sink into her pussy inch by inch. Once I'm fully seated, she lets out a shuttered breath. I pause a moment allowing her to get used to me being deep inside her. "I want you like this every day," I say, my voice ragged as I begin to move. "You feel that?" I pull out and push back in with one long stroke. "You feel how perfect we are together?" Sofia's breath hitches, and she nods.

"Only you."

"Damn straight, only me." I thrust again, causing her to cry out in pleasure. I keep my pace slow and steady while watching her come apart in my arms. My girl has more passion than she ever thought she could. Passion that's only for me. I watch how her eyes drink in every inch of our joined bodies. I watch how she runs her soft, delicate hands up my chest, every touch having a purpose. Like she's locking away images, cataloging them in her brain and allowing them to push away the remnants of the bad memories from her past.

With Sofia clinging to my shoulders and the sound of our harsh breathing echoing off the walls, our bodies move together in perfect harmony. Neither one of us is in a hurry for this moment to end. With our faces a mere inch apart, I feel her breath fan across my lips. With each forward thrust, her hard nipples scrape against my chest. The added friction causes her pussy to flutter around my cock. Bringing her arms above her head, I place my hands in hers, linking our fingers together. I pull out and pause a moment while leaving only the tip inside before sinking back in slowly. "Fuck," I hiss burying my face in the curve of her neck. "So fuckin' wet, so tight," I repeat the process, loving the way her pussy hugs my dick.

"Sam," Sofia pants. "Faster. Please."

Pulling out, I rest my heavy dick wet with her juices along her slit and tease her swollen clit by rubbing it with the head of my cock. "Slow, Firefly. I want to savor every second I'm inside you," I say, pushing back inside her tight heat at the same time I dip down and capture her nipple in my mouth.

"Oh!" she cries, circling her hips making me go deeper; the sensation causes me to growl.

"You keep moving like that, and I'm going to come."

Smiling, she ignores my comment and circles her hips again. This time it's Sofia who is brought to the edge as her pussy becomes even wetter as it clamps down on my cock. Feeling my balls draw up, I give in to my orgasm as the vice-like grip Sofia's pussy has on my dick brings me to the edge. With our hands still joined above our heads, I dominate her lips with mine as I thrust one last time. Planting myself deep inside her, we come together while I absorb her cries with my mouth.

Releasing our hold on each other, Sofia wraps her arms around my back, pulling my body flush against hers and burying her face in the crook of my neck. She lets out a deep breath, and her body begins to shutter. I'm about to ask if she is cold when I feel tears spilling out on my skin. Alarmed, I pull back to find Sofia silently crying. "Baby? Sofia, baby, did I do something wrong? Did I hurt you?" I ask my gut clenching.

She shakes her head. "You didn't do anything wrong," she sniffs. "Just the opposite. You did everything right. I never thought I could feel this way. I never thought I could be with a man and experience what we just had. Then I met you. We became friends and soon after, I started having all these feelings; feelings I was unsure of but wanted to explore." She takes another deep breath trying to compose herself before she continues. "The first time you kissed me on the boat. I knew then I was waiting for the right person, for the right man."

Placing one palm underneath her, cradling her head and the other cupping her cheek, I use the pad of my thumb to wipe away her tears. "I knew the moment I first laid eyes on you while you were standin' by the lake watching the fireflies you were going to be mine. One look into your beautiful eyes and I was fuckin' done. You're in my soul, baby. I love you, Firefly."

"I love you too, Sam."

12

SOFIA

My relationship with Sam is blooming into so much more than I dreamed. I'm finding myself and making my way through life and want to do it all with him by my side. I've caught the wind in my sails. I couldn't be happier, but... It always seems like there is a *but* in there somewhere. Now, I'll be the first to say being a part of The King family is the best thing to ever happen to me, but it feels like every time the dust settles from one problem, another storm begins to brew. Things with this stranger in town that no one can find has my family on high alert and the women here at the house walking on eggshells. Emma seems to be faring okay with everything. It's Luna I worry about. She was starting to open up and socialize. Now, she only leaves her room to use the bathroom and eat. I wish I could stay home with her and help her feel more at ease, but I can't.

Standing in front of my full-length mirror, I run a brush through my hair. The reflection staring back at me is not the same woman I was a couple of days ago. To be honest, a little of that has to do with Sam making love to me. Closing my eyes, I reflect on that moment and get head to toe tingles with the memories of Sam's touch. I open my eyes, looking at myself again. The truth is I'm the reason I feel different. I feel like I'm standing a little taller and have more confidence in myself. Every bit of those feelings comes from the strength within me. I spoke my truth. Owned my past and all the ugly I deal with every day because of it. I feel like I took back a piece of myself when I shared my history with Sam then willingly gave myself to him.

My voice.

My choice.

A light knock on the bedroom door pulls me from my thoughts. "Babe, you ready?" Sam asks from the other side. Setting the hairbrush on top of the dresser, I cross the room and open the door. The first thing I notice is the white paper bag in his hand.

"I didn't hear you leave." Reaching out, I try to grab it from him, but he pulls it back.

"Not even a good morning kiss? I'm hurt." He grabs his chest pretending to be in pain while smirking. "You would pass up these lips for a chocolate croissant?" he teases.

"Depends." I run my fingers along the seam of his open cut.

Sam steps closer. The smell of chocolate mixed with the scent of his cologne invades my senses. "On what?" He raises a curious brow.

Tilting my head to the side, I look at him. "How good it is," I challenge.

Grasping the back of my neck, Sam crashes his lips down on mine, turning my body into an inferno. Once he effectively makes my mind go blank and my knees weak, he pulls away. "Good enough for you?" He gives a cocky grin.

So good. I don't tell him this. I shrug. "I was distracted by hunger. Maybe we should try that again after I eat." As I brush past him, I snag the bag from his hand but don't get far before he pulls me back flush against his body. Dipping his head, he whispers in my ear. The warmth of his breath causes my skin to prickle.

"Maybe we need a repeat of the other night." Sam nips my neck, and my eyes flutter. "I'll feast on your body." Cupping my ass, he squeezes. "When I sink into you, I'll make you forget everything but my name on your lips," he says with all the confidence in the world.

Forget the croissant.

Just as fleeting as my thoughts, Sam releases me. "The crew is waiting on my orders for the day. I'll follow you to work as soon as I'm done, so you should have plenty of time to take care of that hunger of yours." He smiles, knowing he outplayed me. I narrow my eyes to slits. He's playing dirty.

Touché. I stand there in the hallway with nothing more to say.

Kissing my forehead, Sam steps around me and strides down the hall, leaving me wanting him. *Asshole.* But he is mine. That thought alone brings the smile back to my face. "Mornin' Emma," I hear him say, prompting me to turn around to see Emma standing by the bathroom.

Once Sam disappears through the kitchen, Emma whispers, "Girl, that was so hot I think I need a cold shower." She fans herself.

"You and me both," I mumble as I pass by her making my way to the kitchen.

ONCE SAM FILLED his crew in on what needed to be done today while Grey was sitting outside the house, keeping an eye on things, I left for work. I hate that Sam has to follow me everywhere. I kind of feel like it's not necessary, but this is how the club does things when they don't know if there is a threat to someone's safety. As of today, they haven't determined either way if there is anything to worry about. So for now, wherever I go, Sam follows.

"You have a bodyguard today?" Amy greets as she steps out of her car. I look over my shoulder to where Sam has parked his bike.

"Yeah, someone has been snooping around the house, and they haven't found the guy," I explain to Amy.

"You have a crazy life, Sof."

I sigh. She has no idea.

"How are you feeling? The other day at Bella's was pretty intense."

"Much better. I hate you had to see me like that, Amy."

She smiles then looks past my shoulder. "Uh, I'm gonna head inside." I glance behind me, noticing Sam heading our way. "You look happy, Sof. That's all that matters," she tells me as she walks up the steps and into her family's restaurant.

"Keys, babe. Looks like rain, so I'll keep watch from your car until lunch." Sam holds out his hand, and I drop my keys in his palm. The sky above us rumbles with the sound of thunder, and a small drop of rain lands on my cheek. "Get inside before the bottom falls out." He kisses me.

For it to be a stormy day, the restaurant stays busy. When lunchtime rolls around, I'm ready for a break. "Hey, Amy. You ready for lunch?" I ask her on my way toward the back of the kitchen.

"Can't. Jennifer wasn't feeling well and just left, so I have to wait until you get back to take my break."

I hesitate to take my apron off. "You need me to stay?"

Her mom pulls a large pan of hot rolls from the oven. "You go on, sweetie. Take that man of yours who's been sitting outside all day something to eat." She grabs a couple of take-home trays and fills them with coleslaw, fried fish, a roll, and a freshly baked chocolate chip cookie. "These will be waiting for you."

"Thanks, Carol." I head toward the breakroom. After clocking out for lunch, I stop by the restroom. While in the stall, I hear someone walk in. Finished, I step out and find the bathroom empty. *Weird.* I go about my business and wash my hands. The hairs on the back of my neck stand on end and a feeling of unease comes over me. I get the unwelcome feeling of being watched. Suddenly, the lights go out, and my heart jumps into my throat. I go to move in the direction of the bathroom door when the low creak of one of the stalls halts my movement. Flight mode kicks in, but before I'm able to reach the door, a large hand roughly covers my mouth and nose. I want to scream, but the grip the stranger has over my face is so tight I'm finding it hard to draw air. His other hand yanks hard on my ponytail causing my scalp to burn and my eyes to water from the pain. The man reeks of cigarettes and booze. The smell is so strong; it makes me think of Antonio.

"You tell that bitch Luna I'm comin' for her. And you tell your biker friends if they know what's good for them, they'll stay out of my way when I do." His hot putrid breath touches my skin as he whispers his menacing threat into my ear. He runs his tongue along the flesh of my neck and tears pool in my eyes.

No. Not again. I try to scream once more, but my sounds come out muffled, and he tightens his hold completely, blocking my airways to where I have no way of drawing in another breath. I panic. My lungs begin to burn as I struggle against his hold.

"I'll kill you and anyone else who gets in my way," he hisses.

My vision begins to fade. I can feel myself about to pass out. Just as I feel my senses teetering on the edge of blacking out and my body becomes weightless, the man tosses me like I'm nothing more than a piece of trash. I hit the wall, my head smacking hard against the tiles. I'm too busy gasping for air and seeing stars, I don't hear him leave. I lose it. Right there on the bathroom floor, I break down and cry. My head begins to throb from where it smacked against the wall. Suddenly, the bathroom door bursts open allowing the light from the hallway to shine in, and the overhead lighting is turned on. Hearing a loud gasp, I look up.

"Oh my god! Honey, are you okay?" An older lady rushes toward me. I don't know who she is. She looks down at me. "I'll go get the manager. Stay still." She turns and leaves. Within seconds Carol rushes in.

"Sofia." She kneels in front of me. I notice the lady who came in before standing toward the entrance on her phone. Carol turns toward Amy, who slides to a halt after bursting through the bathroom door. "Go get Sam—now," she orders. Looking back at me, she brushes my hair from my face. "Who did this to you?" Anger fills her eyes as her motherly touch accesses my injuries. My head hurts, so I bring my hand to the back of my head which is sore to the touch. My hair feels wet. Pulling my hand away, I look down finding my fingertips coated with blood.

"Sweet Jesus, baby girl." Carol snatches a paper towel from the dispenser above my head and applies pressure. Taking a better look, she tells me, "You have a small laceration and a damn good knot forming. Who did this?" she asks again.

"I don't know." Just as the words leave my mouth, Sam rushes in. His face falls the moment his eyes land on mine, and my lips tremble as tears roll down my cheeks again. He drops to his knees beside Carol, his hands touching me everywhere, looking for injuries.

"Baby." He cups my face, making me focus on him. He wipes the tears away with the pad of his thumb. I blink fresh ones from my lashes. "Does anything hurt?"

I nod. "My head."

"She has a gash along with a bump on the back of her head. The bleeding has stopped, but I'm worried. She should be checked to rule out a concussion," Carol tells Sam. I trust her judgment. She was a nurse for many years before opening the restaurant.

"An ambulance is on the way," Amy mentions.

"I need to shut the place down for the day." Carol places my hand over the paper towel she has pressed against my cut. "Keep the pressure on it until the paramedics get here." She then faces Sam. "Sit with her. Keep her talking. If she has a concussion, we don't want her falling asleep."

"Yes, ma'am," Sam replies.

Carol ushers a few lingering customers out, leaving only me and Sam in the bathroom. I'm in disbelief that this has happened to me. At work of all places. How in the world could someone get in and out without anyone noticing?

"Babe, before EMS gets here, I need you to talk to me. Tell me what happened."

Taking a deep breath, I tell him everything. Right down to the rough, grating sound of his voice to the way he smelled. Before I realize it, I'm shivering. "Women are supposed to feel safe at New Hope House. This man knows Luna is living there. He made it clear he will stop at nothing to get her. She's in danger." I hear faint sirens and look toward the door knowing the ambulance will be here soon. "I'm so sorry I can't tell you what he looked like."

"I won't let anything happen to you again, Sofia. I'm so fuckin' sorry I let it happen this time."

"It's not your fault."

"Yes. It is. I failed you. I'm supposed to watch out for you, and this guy slipped by me somehow."

We hear footsteps just before EMT's enter the bathroom. After a quick assessment, they ask me if I want to go to the hospital. The cut on my head is no longer bleeding, but they strongly recommend I get checked out. I feel okay. A little sore from hitting the wall and a minor headache, but I'll live. Knowing I have Bennett, Mila, or Emerson to call and Sam to watch over me, I decline further treatment. Sam helps me stand. "Please take me home," I tell him.

"Let's get you out of here."

I watch the ambulance drive away as Sam places the seat belt across my chest. Amy and her mom stand beside the car. Giving me a brief kiss, Sam turns facing Carol. I overhear him explaining to her Jake and the guys will be showing up soon to talk with her. I don't worry about her reaction. She likes The Kings. I watch her nod. Amy bends down wrapping her arms around my shoulders. "I hope they catch the bastard who did this and nail his ass to the wall," she proclaims. I smile at the fierceness of her words. Standing, Amy closes the door. I sit in the car alone for a few minutes as Sam paces back and forth in front of the car with his phone to his ear, most likely reporting everything back to Jake—as he should. Eventually, he rounds the hood, opens the door and lowers himself into the driver's seat.

"Jake and Logan will meet us at the house." He turns the key, starting the engine. I look out the passenger side window to see Amy and her mom wave goodbye as we back out of the parking space. I wave back, feeling awful for all the trouble being dumped at their feet. It's not just me or the women in the house I need to worry about, but them as well. At that thought, I start thinking about Luna. Jake is going to question her. There is no way around it. He's going to want answers. Answers she may not be willing to give him. Hopefully, she will trust me enough to tell me something that could help them find this guy.

It doesn't take long to get home. We find Jake and Logan leaning against the porch railing, waiting for us as we pull into the driveway. They quickly stride across the yard meeting us before we climb out of the car.

"Let me look at you." Jake tips my chin and notices the bruises forming on my face around my mouth and nose from the harsh grip the guy had on me. His eyes darken with anger. My eyes water. "Shit. Don't cry, sweetheart." He pulls me in for a hug. When he releases me, I catch the same angry look on Logan's face and his fists clenching at his sides. I give him a weak smile. Stepping forward, he embraces me.

"We'll find the motherfucker," he promises.

"We need to speak with Luna," I hear Jake insist, and I break from Logan's hold to face him.

"Let me talk with her first?" I ask. "She's skittish around men. I might get more information from her than you can." I look to both Jake and Logan. "There's something else you need to know about Luna, and I'm not sure if Sam thought to tell you." I look at Sam. The look on his face says he didn't mention it. I turn my attention back to Jake. "Luna is deaf."

Jake crosses his arms over his broad chest. "That makes things a little more difficult."

"But she reads lips," I rush to add. "Give me a chance to talk with her first. I already knew she was hiding from someone, an ex, but never asked her about the details."

Jake thinks it over for a moment before he decides. "Alright. Find out what you can, but you stress to her that this fucker has threatened my family."

I give Jake a firm understanding nod then walk toward Sam. He tucks a strand of hair behind my ear. Feeling a weight on my shoulders, I bury my face in his chest, and he tells me, "You got this, Firefly." He's right. I'll do whatever it takes to make sure these women and myself are safe.

Sam, Jake, and Logan follow me inside. I continue my way down the hall toward Luna's room and open the door. I find her sitting on a chair next to the window with a paintbrush in one hand and a pallet full of colors in the other as she stares at the blank canvas in front of her. I ease my way further into her room so that I don't startle her. Sensing my presence, she turns her head my way. She takes in my disheveled state. Matted hair, bruised face, and smudged mascara under my eyes. Her eyes widen, and a gasping sound leaves her mouth hinting at the first sound I have ever heard from her. She places her things on a table beside her and walks toward me. Luna studies my face, then ever so softly touches my shoulder.

"I'm going to be okay," I assure her as I lead the way to her bed, and we sit on the edge together. I face her. "I was attacked at work —by a man," I explain trying to ease my way into the conversation. She nods slowly. I grab her by the hand. "He said he knows who you are. He mentioned you by name." She covers her mouth. Pulling her other hand free from mine, she backs away from me. I get her to look at me again. "He threatened my family and me. I need you to tell me who he is." She shakes her head and shuts her eyes. She's frightened. I get it. I am too. But we need to learn not to let that fear control us. I need to get her to tell me something— anything. I slide closer to her. She lifts her head, tears streaming down her face as I continue to talk. She focuses on my mouth. "Please. Tell me something. We won't let anything happen to you, but I need to be able to tell those men out there—my family a name or a description so they can find this guy," I beg her.

Finally, she nods. Grabbing her notebook, she begins to write. She hands it to me.

What did he look like? It could be any of them. They go by the name Savage Outlaw MC.

"An MC?" I whisper to myself. Then I remember and look at Luna. "I didn't see his face, but would it help if I told you he smelled like he smoked a carton of cigarettes a day and bathed in alcohol?" Recognition shines in her eyes, and I become hopeful. She takes the notebook and scribbles more words.

Pike. He is their VP.

I sag my shoulders and ask, "Luna, how did you get mixed up with these guys?" I hand her notebook back, hoping she will share with me. She does.

I became involved with the President. Stupid. I know. I thought he was a good guy. He treated me nice enough. That all changed when I saw something I shouldn't have. He beat me. Dumped my body on the side of the road and left me for dead. I survived. Now he is sitting in jail until the trial. And I am the key witness.

I read all this. Though she doesn't give me details, it's enough to read between the lines and understand why she is so fearful. Lifting my eyes from the paper, I look at her. "Now, they want to finish the job."

13

SAM

Pacing the living room at Sofia's house, I do my best to rein in my anger. I'm angry because some motherfucker put his filthy hands on my woman, but most of all, I'm angry at myself for letting it happen. I am in charge of keeping her safe. The club trusted me with the task, and in return, I failed them both.

"Sam," Jake's gruff voice calls out, interrupting my personal tirade. "I know you're inside your head right now, and nothing me or anyone else says will make a difference, but get your shit under control." He points toward the back of the house, where Sofia disappeared a few minutes ago. "Your woman doesn't need you like this. She's going to need you to be the level headed one. Sofia may be holding up well now, but this shit is going to hit hard later, and when it does, she'll need you to get her through it. You got me?"

I run my hand down my face. "Yeah, I got you. You're right. It's just that I fucked up. I fucked up, and my girl paid for it. That bastard marked her; made her bleed, Jake." I shake my head. "I want the son of a bitch to pay."

"Oh, he'll pay," Jake declares. "Now, take all the fire burnin' inside your belly and focus that energy on how you plan on makin' it happen."

Just then, Sofia appears from the back of the house with Luna in tow. She hovers behind Sofia while refusing to make eye contact with me, Jake or Logan. She's afraid of us. I don't know if it's because we are male or because of our cuts. I look over at Jake and Logan to see they've made the same assessment. Sofia is the first to speak. "I want to start by saying you know how New Hope House operates. We don't turn any woman away no matter what their past is. We also don't force them to tell us their stories. I know first hand how difficult opening up can be." At Sofia's admission, Jake's and Logan's features soften. "My number one priority is making sure the women who stay here are safe. The second is helping them start over and rebuild their lives. Luna is no exception, except for today. Today I had to break one of my rules and ask Luna to share why she came here. She is terrified, but because of my attack, she is more than willing to give you whatever information you want. I'm going to start by telling you what she has already told me. If you have any more questions, she is prepared to answer."

Jake nods. "Alright, sweetheart. Tell us what you know."

Sofia and Luna take a seat on the sofa. Luna is visibly shaking. Sofia reaches over and takes her hand, offering support. "Luna's ex's name is Rex. He's also the president of the Savage Outlaw MC." Sofia drops the bomb. One we sure as hell wasn't expecting.

"Son of a fuckin' bitch," Jake hisses the same time "fuck" escapes both mine and Logan's mouth. When our body language causes a panicked look to strike Luna's face, Sofia urges her to look at her and read her lips.

"It's okay. Nobody here is going to hurt you. The Kings are not like that. I promise." Luna closes her eyes and nods frantically as she gets her fear under control.

"Was it her ex that attacked you?" I ask.

"No. Luna says he's in jail awaiting trial."

"Trial for what?" Logan questions.

"Murder. Luna witnessed the whole thing. She is supposed to testify against him. She believes it was Pike, Rex's brother, who attacked me."

"He's sending a message to Luna through you," I state.

"Yes. I believe he wanted to scare me into kicking Luna out of New Hope House. Pike knows about you guys. I think he assumes Luna is under The Kings' protection as well."

Jake interjects. "The prick was bankin' on roughin' you up would be enough for us to send the girl packin'. If we send her on her way, that makes their job of snatching her up easier."

Sofia looks from me to Jake then to Logan. "I'm not turning my back on Luna."

My girl is so damn brave. I knew that's what she'd say. I'd say by the look on Jake's face he knew as well. Stepping in front of the sofa where Luna and Sofia sit, Jake crouches down to eye level. He cocks his head to the side waiting for Luna to look at him. When her scared eyes finally meet his, he speaks slowly to allow Luna to read his lips. "You mean somethin' to Sofia, so that means you mean somethin' to the club. You are under The Kings' protection." Jake turns his attention to Sofia. "Tell us everything she knows about Savage Outlaw."

Roughly an hour later, Luna and Sofia have finished relaying every piece of information Luna knows about her ex, his brother and their club. Jake didn't waste any time getting on his phone and ordering Grey and Blake over here. He's ordered Sofia, Emma, and Luna to stay at the clubhouse until we can get a better handle on the situation. The club is not willing to take any risks, especially now that we know we are dealing with another MC. Hearing the rumble of two Harleys outside, Jake turns to Logan and me. "Let's go. Church in thirty. Grey and Blake are going to help Sofia and the other two women pack."

Standing, Sofia makes her way over to me. I wrap my arms around her. "You holding up okay, baby?"

"I'm doing okay, Sam. I need to stay strong for Luna. She knows we have been ordered to stay at the clubhouse, and that scares her. It will take some time, but she'll soon see The Kings are nothing like her ex."

I kiss her lips. "I want you to be strong for a little while longer; then tonight, I want you to let it all go while I hold you."

Sofia takes a deep breath. "Deal."

I kiss her one last time. "When you get to the clubhouse, I want you to unpack in my room."

She smiles. "Okay."

When we are about half a mile from the compound, I spot Gabriel, Reid, and Quinn in my side mirror riding up behind us. Letting off the throttle, I allow them to take their place in the formation behind Jake and Logan. A short ride later, we pull through the compound gates parking outside the clubhouse. Not a word is spoken as we follow Jake inside and to the room church is held. Getting down to business Jake slams the gavel. "You've been made aware of the fact Sofia was attacked at work this afternoon." The atmosphere in the room turns deadly at the news. "The piece of shit that roughed her up made it clear his message was for Luna, the young woman staying at New Hope House." Jake pauses before he delivers the next blow knowing it's about to set shit off. "It's lookin' like Luna has gotten herself mixed up with an MC—Savage Outlaw. More specifically, their Prez. She witnessed some shit not meant for her eyes. Because of this, some pussy known as Rex beat her from an inch of her life, dumped her body out in the middle of nowhere, leaving her for dead. The problem for his club is Luna didn't die and is now the only witness to a murder he's currently sittin' in jail for. Now I didn't ask for the details on what she saw because it's not of any relevance to us, so for right now, our only focus is on finding the club's VP Pike who happens to be Rex's brother. He's the one who got to Sofia."

"Fuck, Prez. Was she his old lady?" Quinn asks.

"No. Luna said she hadn't been seein' Rex for very long, and she knew he was in an MC but was never brought into the fold. She had no clue her man was into some heavy shit."

"I've never heard of this club," Logan adds. "What about you, Prez? Got any idea who we're about to tangle with?"

"Not really. No more than a few whispers here and there over the years. Not enough to give me an opinion on what kind of men they are, but seeing how they have no qualms putting their hands on a woman, that says all I need to know about them," Jake grinds out.

"Sam, you didn't see nothin' while you were waitin' outside Sofia's work?" Quinn questions and I shake my head.

"No. Not a damn thing. Nobody matching Sofia's description walked into The Pier."

"I got the security feed," Reid breaks in. "You are not going to believe this shit, Prez," Reid clicks on his keyboard, and a video pops up on the TV in the corner of the room. "Sam was right. The fucker didn't slip past him. Sam never saw him because the pussy broke in before the restaurant opened." Fuck. Reid is right. We all watch as Pike breaks in through the back exit by the dumpster. Next, Reid brings up the footage of the inside of the restaurant. He fast forwards the video and stops on the part where we watch Sofia walk into the restroom. Several seconds later, Pike slips in. Reid pauses the video. There are no cameras in the bathroom, but we know what went down behind those doors. I want to put my hands around the fucker's neck and squeeze the life out of him. I now understand what it's like to love someone so fiercely you'd kill for them.

"Prospect!" Jake barks so loud his voice vibrates off the walls of the room. His expression says he's been calling my name, but I've been too inside my head to hear him.

"Sorry, sir."

Jake gives me a pointed look. "There is not one brother sittin' at this table that hasn't been in your shoes, Sam. Each one of us knows what it's like to see our woman hurt; to witness evil creep in and try to destroy what's most important to us. We've also been in a situation where we've felt helpless and blamed ourselves for not protecting them when they needed us. But at the end of the day, you have to suck it up and come to terms with that shit. The club is depending on you to keep a level head. Your brothers depend on you to have their back. And know in return they will have yours." Jake pauses a moment, letting his words sink in. He's right. No matter what situation I'm faced with, I need to keep myself in control and my head clear. When Jake sees the clarity in my eyes, he nods and continues. "Today was not your fault. I would not have let you be the one to watch over Sofia had I not believed in your ability to do so." Jake points to the TV on the wall. "That asshole snuck in hours before opening and slipped out the moment you went in to check on Sofia. He calculated his moves and knew how not to get caught."

"What's our next move?" this coming from Reid.

"I want you to find out everything you can on this Savage Outlaw MC. I want to know about their Prez and the charges against him as well and when his next court date is. Luna mentioned she wasn't sure she was going to go back home to testify against him. With Rex's men after her, I don't see her riskin' her life to take the stand. But I got a plan brewin' to solve that problem. I'll clue you all in once I've ironed out my execution." Next, Jake turns his attention to Gabriel. "I want you and Sam to hit the streets. Scour the area around where Sofia works, talk to the locals, find out if they've seen anyone wearin' a cut not belonging to The Kings. Also, head on out to Charley's and ask him if he's seen anything."

"What are we doin' about Sofia and the ladies stayin' at New Hope House?" Quinn asks.

"Blake and Grey are bringin' them here. I want them to be watched around the clock. I won't be puttin' the club on lockdown just yet. Right now, the only threat has been to Sofia and Luna. If things escalate further, we'll bring our women and children in. Make sure you tell your old ladies to stay vigilant. I also want all of you on the road as much as possible. Drive around and make your presence known. You know the drill, now get it done." Jake slams the gavel.

Striding out of church, I follow Gabriel outside to our bikes. Straddling his bike, Gabriel lights a cigarette. "Let's hit up Charley's first."

Once the two of us hit Main Street, we ride side by side in the direction of Polson's local bar. Flying toward us in the opposite direction are two men on bikes. Gabriel and I look at each other, and I know he's made the same assessment as me. Both men are wearing cuts. When Gabriel reaches into his cut, retrieving his gun, I follow his lead and do the same. He motions down giving me the signal he's planning to take out their tires. With a lift of my chin, I acknowledge his plan of attack. With my heart pumping and my adrenalin racing through my veins, I raise my pistol. I let thoughts of Sofia and her bruised face run through my head as I pull the trigger. Mine and Gabriel's shots ring out and effectively take out both bikes. The sound of screeching metal fills the air around us as both bikes skid across the asphalt before landing in a ditch on the side of the road. Rolling up to the wreckage, Gabriel and I climb off our bikes with our pistol's still drawn as we approach the two misfortunate assholes whose day is about to get a whole lot worse. One guy appears to be unconscious as the other tries to pick himself up off the ground. Striding toward him, I kick, landing a solid blow to the side of his head with my steel toe boot, knocking him out. Gabriel grunts and nods as he brings his phone to his ear. "Hey, Prez. Need a cage. We're about two miles out from Charley's."

"What now?" I ask.

Gabriel grins. "Now, we get to have some fun."

Pulling alongside our bikes on the side of the road, Quinn jumps out of the van. "You rang?" he sing songs as he makes his way to where Gabriel and I are standing. "Goddamn, that's some serious road rash," he whistles while inspecting the side of one guy's face. "Well, let's get these fuckers loaded."

Back at the clubhouse, I lean against the wall down in the basement of the clubhouse. I watch while Gabriel and Logan strap the two Savage Outlaw men to chairs. Both men are still gagged and have hoods covering their heads. A second later, the door opens, and the creaking sound of the stairs alerts us to Jake's arrival.

"What ya thinkin', Prez?" Logan asks.

Jake looks down at his watch then at us. "It's gettin' close to supper time. Grace will have my balls if I miss eatin' with the girls two days in a row." He smirks. "Sam, Gabriel," he jerks his chin. "Let them chill in the freezer a bit."

Without hesitation, I grab the back of one chair as Gabriel does the same with the other. The legs of the metal chairs grind against the concrete floor as we pull them into the industrial-size walk-in freezer on the opposite side of the basement. The guy I'm pulling begins to grunt and thrash around in his seat. Raising my left arm, I bring my elbow down against his jaw, knocking him out once again.

14

SOFIA

With Sam gone, I walk down the hallway with Luna. I know the best place for us, to keep us safe, is the clubhouse, but convincing the other women is another story. I don't want Luna or Emma to be afraid. I want them to trust me, and I want both to trust the rest of my family as well.

Opening the door to Luna's room, I turn to her, and she stares at me. "I'll help you pack a few things."

Luna hangs her head, and her pen glides across the paper. *I'm sorry. I didn't mean to cause trouble. I should leave.*

I shake my head; that is not going to happen. "No. The Kings will do whatever it takes to keep you safe and find this guy." A soft knock on Luna's bedroom door draws my attention. The door opens, and Emma appears.

"Hey." She notices the mood in the room as her eyes drift from me to Luna. She steps in, pushes the door closed, and leans her back against it. Emma motions over her shoulder with her thumb. "Did you know there are a couple of bikers sitting in our living room?"

"About that—" I go to say more, but Emma interrupts.

"Jesus, Sofia." She advances toward Luna and me, her attention trained on my face. "What the hell happened?" she takes in the bruises I have yet to look at.

"I was attacked at work by a man trying to get to Luna," I tell her. Emma's eyes dart to Luna then back to me. "That explains the reason those men are here. Is this connected to the creep caught casing the house?" she asks.

I nod. "Yes. The Kings believe it's the same person." Sighing, I let her know, "Austin and Grey are waiting for us to pack our bags. We're staying at The Kings' clubhouse where they can keep us safe until they find this guy."

Emma frowns. "Leave the house? What about work? I just started this job. I don't know, Sofia. Not that I think badly of The Kings, but I don't know about staying at their clubhouse."

I turn to Luna. Her face is cast down, looking at her paper as she absently drags her pen across the pages making loops and lines. Lifting my chin, I look back at Emma. "It's the only way to keep us safe, Emma. This guy is after Luna, and he made it clear he is willing to hurt anyone standing in his way." I can tell she is unsure, but she finally agrees.

After we help Luna pack a bag, she follows Emma down the hall and into her room, while I step across the hall into mine. Digging around in the top of my closet, I find the bookbag I used while in school. Only packing a few outfits and a couple pairs of shoes, I leave my room and head down the hall to the bathroom. Turning the light on, I grab my toothbrush and other personal products I will need. I pause, finally looking at myself in the mirror. Lifting my hand, I brush my fingers across the red and purple marks on my skin, then run my fingers through my hair. *Never thought I'd see myself look like this again.* Grabbing a hair tie off the countertop, I gather my hair and create a loose braid as I continue to stare at my reflection. I haven't seen bruises on any part of my body in a long time. I wore them almost every day when Los Demonios imprisoned me. Antonio roughed me up often. He got off on hurting me. Memories of his heavy hand slapping my face surface to the forefront of my mind.

"We're all set and ready to go." Emma appears in the doorway with Luna standing behind her. Taking a deep breath, I clear my mind of my ugly past.

"Let's go tell the guys." Moving to the side, they let me lead the way as the three of us enter the living room, with our bags in our hands. Austin and Grey stand. Grey's eyes fall on Emma, looking at her the same way Sam looks at me, causing her to step a bit closer to my side. Luna stands on my other side and stares ahead, waiting for one of them to speak.

"Sofia," Austin speaks. "I want the three of you to follow Grey in your car, and I'll fall behind you. We stay that way until we get through the gate at the clubhouse."

"Wait a minute. I need my car," Emma interjects.

Grey shakes his head. I already know how this is going to go. "We've got our orders. You need to go somewhere; I'll take you and bring you back."

Emma's mouth falls open, but she remains silent. Austin opens the front door and waits for us to step outside, then sets the alarm. Emma, Luna, and I place our bags in the back seat behind the driver's side, before climbing in. Both ladies including myself, fall silent and wait for Grey. Once he pulls his bike onto the road, I back out and pull up behind him. Austin falls in behind my car. I know the routine. I've been through it a few times over the past couple of years.

We ride in silence for a short time before Emma speaks. "So, what's it going to be like at The Kings of Retribution clubhouse? I mean, since living in Polson I've heard people in town talk about things. On the other hand, they are your family, and I know you hang out there often. Is it true they have women who live there—for sexual purposes?"

Crap. I forgot about Ember and Raine. "The club has two club girls —Ember and Raine. And yes, if they choose to have sex with a member, they do. I know what you've heard around town. I've heard it too." I shake my head. "The Kings are good to them. They don't hurt women or force them to do things against their will. Raine and Ember are good people, Emma. They are part of the family too." We pull off the main highway onto the dirt road leading to the clubhouse, and I glance over my shoulder at Emma. "I didn't know what to expect at first when I came out here for the first time. My experience with bikers before meeting The Kings was not a good one, but I knew from the first moment I met these men, I would have nothing to be afraid of." I smile her way. "Go in there with an open mind."

Emma picks at the hem of her skirt. I can tell that she is nervous. Lifting my eyes, I peer in the rearview mirror and peek at Luna, who is sitting in the back seat. Holding tight to the duffle bag sitting on her lap, she stares out the window, her face void of any emotion. I can tell right away she has drawn back into herself. I slow the car as we pull up to the gate at the end of the property. Pulling his bike up next to my car and alongside the intercom, Blake punches the security code in the keypad, and the massive metal gate starts to slide open. Emma turns her head from left to right. "Does this fencing go around the entire property?"

"I believe so. You've seen the security system at the house." I turn my head in her direction just as we begin to move, and she nods. "Keeping the family safe is important to the club."

"I'd say so. Looks like the perimeter of a state prison," Emma mumbles.

Gravel crunches beneath the tires of my car as we leave the dirt road and enter the main compound area of the club. Blake and Grey pull their bikes up to the front where the members park, and I drive around to the opposite side parking just under the tree closest to the building where most of the old ladies tend to park.

"Well, here we are. Home sweet home—for now anyway." I try to make light of the situation.

Grey walks up to the car just as we've unbuckled and opens Emma's door at the same time Blake opens the door for Luna. "Blake and I will carry your things inside." His eyes shift from Emma to me as we step out of the car. I notice Luna's body language as she stiffens. Blake gives me a look. Lifting his chin, he motions for me to walk around to the passenger side.

"Why don't you help her. She flinched when I went to reach for her bag. I don't want to scare her more than she already is. It's got to be hard as fuck not being able to hear shit around you on top of being frightened like she is," he says. "Fuckin bullshit, man. No woman should fear a man like that."

"The motherfucker who made her that way needs his ass beat," Grey remarks as he grabs mine and Emma's bags from the back seat.

Squatting, I get Luna to look at me. "Come on." I grab her hand and smile. "You got this." She climbs out of the car. Luna looks from Grey to Blake. Giving them a weak smile, she signs the word sorry and hands her bag to Blake. "She said sorry," I tell him. Blake looks her way and nods.

"Let's get you, ladies, inside. Follow me, and I'll show you to your rooms." Grey turns and heads toward the door.

I keep hold of Luna's hand, and Emma walks in front of me as Grey leads us inside. It takes a moment for my eyes to adjust from the bright sun to the dim lighting as we step through the front door of the clubhouse. "I'll give you guys a tour of the place once we get settled, but this is the common area. It's where all the members and sometimes the family hang out. As you can tell there is a bar over there," I point to my right, "and pool tables, seating scattered about on the opposite side over there," I motion to my left as we make our way across the room toward the stairs leading to the second floor. "All the rooms are located upstairs." Both Emma and Luna take everything in as we pass.

Once we are shown to our rooms, the guys leave us to get settled. With my bag in my hand, I push the door open, entering Sam's bedroom. It looks like the other rooms in the clubhouse. Crossing the room, I toss my bag on the bed. At the sound of a soft knock, I look over my shoulder to find Raine standing inside the open door.

"Hey, Sofia," she says, walking in.

"Hey, Raine." Her face shows concern when her eyes fall on my bruises but she says nothing about them.

"I wanted to introduce myself to our guest and maybe help them get settled, see if you guys needed anything."

"That sounds like a great idea." Walking out of the room, we cross the hall to where Emma will sleep. Her door is open, so Raine and I walk in. Emma steps out of the small bathroom. She takes in Raine's appearance; tattoos, short denim skirt, black tank top, and black biker boots. Raine has a badass edgy look to her, but she is one of the kindest people I know.

"Emma, meet Raine," I introduce the two. Emma gives her a friendly smile.

"It's nice to meet you."

"You too. I'm totally diggin' your style. The whole retro pinup girl look is sexy." Raine complements Emma's appearance. Emma looks down at herself, smoothing her hands down the front of her red body-hugging pencil skirt.

"I've never looked at myself as sexy. Never had someone tell me so either."

Raine looks shocked. "Well, you fuckin' should think that way because you are smokin' hot," she says, earning another smile from Emma. "Ember, the other club girl; she has a similar style. You should get to meet her soon. She's downstairs in the kitchen whipping up something for you ladies to eat."

"I look forward to it," Emma remarks.

I turn, facing Raine. "Ready to meet Luna?" I say to Raine.

"Yep."

Leaving Emma's room, Raine and I walk two doors down the hall. Luna's door is closed, but before I turn the handle, I explain to Raine, "Luna is deaf. Make sure you face her. That way, she has a clear view of you speaking so she can read your lips. She's quite good at it." Raine nods. Cracking the door open, I poke my head inside to find Luna gazing out the bedroom window. Sensing us, she spins. Luna's big violet eyes stare at us as we cross the room.

"Luna, this is Raine." I motion to my left where Raine is standing. Luna's eyes shift to Raine. Lifting her hand, she gives Raine a small wave.

Lifting her hands, Raine shocks both Luna and me when she starts signing. My mouth falls open, and Luna immediately responds.

"I've known you for two years and never knew you could sign." I'm still amazed and wish I knew how to communicate the same way with Luna, but thankful she has Raine who can help her feel more at ease.

Raine shrugs her shoulders like it's no big deal but keeps signing even when she talks with me, not leaving Luna out of the conversation between us. "I never had a reason to bring it up. My brother is deaf. I learned how to sign alongside him when we were young." I learn another fact about Raine on top of her ability to sign; her brother is deaf. I knew she had a brother, but she has never mentioned specific details about him before.

"Do you mind if I head back to my room? It would be nice to get cleaned up before Sam, and the others get here."

Raine takes a seat on the bed, and Luna sits beside her, finally feeling comfortable. "Go ahead. I'm going to visit with Luna for a bit." She turns to Luna. "Is that okay with you? Can I visit with you awhile?" she speaks and signs. Luna nods. Feeling relief in knowing the women are doing okay with being here, I leave and head back to Sam's room. Closing the door behind me, I grab my bag taking it to the bathroom with me and set it on the counter by the sink. Unzipping it, I pull out a clean outfit setting the pile of clothes on the shelf. Reaching behind the shower curtain, I turn the shower on. As I'm waiting for the water to warm, I dig my personal products like shampoo, lotions and a toothbrush out of my bag and stow them away in the cabinet above the toilet and the shampoo on the shelf inside the shower. Removing the holder from the end of my hair, I run my finger through releasing the braid, then strip my clothes off. Pulling back the curtain, I step into the shower. The moment the hot water hits my skin tension releases and my body relaxes. I stand there for the longest time, with my eyes shut tight, letting the water wash over me. Washing away the dried blood from my hair and washing the filthy touch of my attacker down the drain, ridding myself of the horrible day I have had.

15

SAM

W alking into my room, the first thing I notice is Sofia's bags sitting on my bed. The second thing is the sound of the shower running. The thought of her naked and wet behind the bathroom door has my dick hard as a rock. Sliding my cut off, I lay it across the bed before stripping off my clothes. When Sofia hears the click of the door, she calls out my name. "Sam?"

"It's me, babe." Pulling back the shower curtain, I'm rewarded with Sofia's shy smile as I step inside the shower. I don't waste any time putting my hands on my woman. Wrapping one arm around her waist, I bring her wet body flush against mine and take the kiss I desperately need. Eager for her taste, I run my tongue against the seam of her lips, and she opens for me. The moment her tongue touches mine the need to be inside her intensifies. Overcome with her desperation, Sofia hooks her leg over mine urging me closer. Knowing she's okay with what's happening, I follow her lead. Cupping her ass in my hands, I lift her the same time she wraps her legs around my waist. Bracing her back against the tiled wall, I break our kiss. Reaching between our slick bodies,

I take my cock in my hand and line the head up at her entrance. "Yes?"

"God, yes," she pants. The second the words leave her mouth, I surge forward, burying myself completely inside her tight heat, nearly choking at how incredible her pussy feels hugging my cock. Sofia's nails digging into my back adds fuel to the fire burning inside me. With my hands still gripping her lush, round ass, I begin moving her up and down on my cock. I look down between our joined bodies and watch as I disappear inside her. I glance up at her face to find her doing the same. Both of us getting off at the sight of her perfect pussy taking my cock. I love the look on my girls face as she allows her body to give in to the pleasure, as she uses my body to discover her own. "Look at me," I growl. Sofia's head snaps up, and her hooded eyes connect with mine. Not once do we break our connection as I continue to drive into her. When her thighs tighten around my hips, and her pussy begins to clamp down on my dick signaling her orgasm, I allow myself to let go along with her. With one last thrust, Sofia throws her head back and cries out her release the same moment I bury my face in the crook of her neck getting lost in my own.

As we come down from our high, Sofia's body trembles as she clings to me, unwilling to let go. Turning the water off, I step out of the shower with her in my arms. Snagging the large white towel hanging on a hook on the back of the door, I wrap her wet body with it. I walk out of the bathroom and sit on the edge of the bed. Laying next to me is a navy-blue fleece blanket. Grabbing it, I sling it over my shoulders and wrap mine and Sofia's body in it. I decide to stay silent and wait for my girl to wrap her head around her current feelings. I'm so proud of the way she was able to let go with me moments ago. When she finally lifts her head, I'm rewarded with a drunken, lazy smile, and I can't help but chuckle. "How ya doin', Firefly?"

"That was..." she pauses, trying to find the right words.

"That was what, baby?" I grin.

"That was good," she says, hiding her face against my chest as her cheeks turn pink.

I place my finger under her chin. "Look at me, baby. It was better than good. It was fuckin' great. Don't ever be embarrassed to tell me how you feel or even what you like."

"I don't know what I would like," she confesses in a whisper.

"I know this is all still new, and you're trusting me to take the lead, but one day you'll find yourself wanting to try certain things. And when you do, I want you to share those needs with me so I can give them to you."

"Okay," she agrees, her face turning redder. I know my girl will come out of her shell one day, but for now, there is no rush.

An hour later, I leave a sleeping Sofia in my bed and head back down to the basement. By the time I get there, all the men are standing, waiting for Prez. Within seconds, Jake walks in and closes the door behind him. "Let's get down to business and find out what these cocksuckers have to say."

Taking a seat in a chair placed in the middle of the room, Jake lights a cigarette and waits for Gabriel and Logan to open the door to the cooler. The two men are dragged out and placed in front of him. Jerking his chin, he motions for Logan and Gabriel to remove their hoods. For a minute, I think the two men are dead by the stillness of their bodies and the pale blue shade of their skin and lips. That is until Gabriel picks up a bucket from the corner of the room and dowses both men with water startling them awake. "Wakey, wakey," Quinn teases as he goes to stand next to Jake. This will be my first time being a part of one of The Kings' interrogations. I plan to hold back and keep my trap shut unless instructed otherwise.

"Your piece of shit club made a mistake thinkin' it could come into Kings territory," Jake informs in a calm but lethal tone. "Your second mistake was goin' after one of our old ladies. I'll tell you now there's nothin' and no one that can save you, but you tell me what I want to know, I'll consider showin' you mercy when I end your worthless lives."

"Fuck you," one guy says the same time the second man spits at Jake's' feet. No sooner do the words leave his mouth, Jake is off his chair and lands a punch to the idiots face the same time Quinn lands a solid blow to asshole number two. Those punches send both men and the metal chairs they're sitting on crashing to the floor. The big guy who had the nerve to spit in Jake's direction hits the floor along with an audible thump as his head bounces off the concrete. Showing disrespect toward our Prez earns such action, and what they did to my woman will earn them much more. I don't feel one ounce of remorse toward them. With both men still strapped to the chairs lying on the cold floor of the basement, Jake orders. "Pick their asses up." Gabriel and Logan haul the two men up to face Jake once again. "Tell me where your club is held up at," Jake questions again.

"Doesn't matter what we tell ya," one guy says through a busted mouth. "They'll be gone by the time you get there. With us missin', they will know something is up. Besides." He smirks. "Pike has no intention of leaving Polson without gettin' what he came for. That little bitch Luna will get what's comin' to her. As you know, we have no problem takin' whoever gets in our way. Even pretty little cunts like the one my VP roughed up. Although I can think of some far better things to do with the bitch." The second the words leave the motherfuckers mouth I see red—his blood on my hands. Without a thought, my body moves on autopilot as I fly across the room and tackle the soon-to-be-dead asshole to the floor. Nobody in the room makes a move to stop me as I deliver punch after punch. With my adrenaline pumping along with the image of Sofia's bruised face and the thoughts of these men violating her, I continue my assault. I want the man to stop breathing. When he does, I know he'll never get the chance to hurt my girl again. I don't know how much time has passed, but before I know it, someone hauls me off the guy, and it's Gabriel's gruff voice I hear. "Suficiente *enough,* brother."

Out of breath and my chest heaving, I look down at the unconscious, bloody man at my feet. I then turn my attention to Jake. "Sorry, Jake. It wasn't my place to jump in as I did. It's just..." I pause and shake my head.

"It sure as fuck was your place, son. You reacted the same way anyone of us would if it were our old lady the son of a bitch was carryin' on about."

With his buddy laying out cold on the floor, Jake turns his attention to the other biker. The one who carries a look on his face that says he's finally grasped the magnitude of how fucked he is. "I'm askin' one last time. Where is your club held up?"

"We've been stayin' at an abandoned house the next town over. It's about two miles from the lumber mill on Beasley Road."

Standing from his chair, Jake gives Gabriel a nod, then gives the rest of us men the signal to follow him. Without looking back, I walk out of the basement. The last thing I hear is Gabriel's voice. "Decirle al diablo que dije hola. *Tell the devil I said hello.*"

When we step outside the clubhouse, I close my eyes and take in a much-needed breath of fresh air while I process what took place moments ago. I feel absolutely nothing. *Does that make me fucked up*? As if he's able to read my thoughts, Jake's voice breaks through the fog surrounding me. "If given a chance to do it all again, would you change anything that happened down in that basement? Would you choose to spare their lives knowin' you're riskin' Sofia's or anyone else you care about?"

My answer is immediate. "No." Jake and I hold each other's stare for several beats before he nods and mounts his bike. He then turns toward his brothers, who are waiting for his orders. "Grey and Blake, I want you to stay and help Gabriel with the cleanup. Austin, I want you on watch until we get back. The rest of you come with me."

It doesn't take long before we arrive in the next town over from Polson and drive past the lumber mill. When we reach Beasley Road, we are on high alert, but as expected, the abandoned house appears to be empty. We park on the gravel driveway and peer around the yard. It's littered with garbage and empty beer bottles. "Check around back," Jake orders. With my pistol drawn, I cover Quinn's back as we turn the corner of the house leading to the back yard. We find nothing. Logan steps out on the back porch. "The house is clear. Fuckers ran." Jake steps out of the house next to Logan. "Let's head back to the clubhouse. Not much else we can do tonight with Savage Outlaw in the wind."

Back at the clubhouse, it's 3:00 am, and I am wide awake. My brain is on overload with all that has happened as of late. So much has changed in the past several weeks. I finally got my girl, my father has crawled back under his rock in Texas where he belongs, and I have The Kings, the family I always wanted. But even with all the good, I have this nagging feeling in the pit of my stomach. There is a storm brewing.

16

SOFIA

Rolling over, I lift the blanket covering both Sam and me and move to get out of bed. Before the tips of my toes touch the floor, Sam's strong arm snakes around my waist, pulling me backward. Holding my body snug, my back against his front he buries his face in the crook of my neck. His warm breath sends tingles throughout my body.

"Where do ya think you're going?" His gruff sleepy voice sounds sexy as hell, and I wiggle my backside against him.

"I had planned on letting you sleep while I grabbed a shower." I feel his hand slip from my waist, his fingertips drawing a path over the curve of my hip, down my thigh, before dragging it back up my body. He kisses my neck, causing my eyes to flutter shut and my body to hum with anticipation of him giving me more.

"I like waking up to you in my bed," he confesses.

"I like it too," I moan when his fingertips slip beneath my panties. I gasp as he slowly rubs circles on my clit.

"I love the way your body responds to me, Firefly." His hips press into my back while he rubs his length against me as he continues to work my nub. A burning ache builds between my legs, and my breath hitches the closer he brings me to the edge of climaxing. Just as my body is on the verge of coming, he stops.

"Sam." My breaths come out like wisps of air. "Please."

Bringing his body over mine, he dips his head and takes my mouth with his. Desperate for more, I pull him closer, wanting to feel the weight of his body against mine. I pour everything I'm feeling for him into our kiss. I have fallen so hard for this man.

Feeling the weight of his arousal against my thigh, I part my legs, letting him settle between them. Never breaking our kiss, Sam enters me in one slow motion. My hands slip over his shoulders and down his back. Gripping his ass in both my hands, I dig my nails into his flesh, urging him to give me more. Hiking my leg over his hip, he gives me what I want.

Once again, my climax builds. Grinding down, Sam creates the perfect amount of friction against my sensitive bundle of nerves, just enough to send me over the edge. Waves of intense pleasure ripple throughout my body. I feel another orgasm build on the backside of the one he just gave me. In one fluid motion, he flips us, bringing me to settle on top of him without breaking our connection.

"Ride me, babe." His hands grasp my hips, guiding my movements, helping me find my rhythm. His eyes fall to where we are connected, and they stay there. Using the pad of his thumb, he rubs my clit. I feel my walls tighten around his shaft with every stroke.

"Oh my god." My toes curl as tension builds.

"That's it. Give me one more, beautiful." With those words, I'm gone. My orgasm explodes. Gripping my hips, Sam thrusts his hips upward a few times finding his own release.

Still sensitive, I tremble as he slips from beneath me and tucks me into his side. Wrecked, I lay there as Sam continues to hold me. With my body draped over him, I let the steady rise and fall of his chest soothe me. The last thing I remember before falling asleep is the deep timbre of his voice saying, "Sleep, baby. I got you."

AFTER SHOWERING AND GETTING DRESSED, I follow Sam downstairs straight into the kitchen, where we find Lisa cooking alongside Ember. Emma and Luna are already eating breakfast at the kitchen table with Raine. I watch her and Luna's interaction. Their hands move as they communicate with each other. The fact that Raine knows sign language helps make this whole experience a little easier on Luna.

"Hey, you two," Lisa greets us. "Come on over here and fix you a plate while it's hot." As Sam and I load our plates, Grey strides in through the sliding door leading to the backyard. I take my plate to the table and sit on the other side of Luna. Turning her body, she looks at me and smiles.

"You look like you are feeling better today," I smile back, instead of using her notepad, Luna signs, as Raine translates.

"Much better, thank you."

Sam pulls the chair from the table. Grey does the same taking a seat next to Emma. "Prez gave the go-ahead on taking you ladies to town since the two of you have doctor appointments, and since you may need a few more things from the house, we'll be stopping by there too," Grey mentions before lifting a fork full of the pancake to his mouth.

Luna wasn't looking at Grey when he spoke, so Raine tells her what he had to say. Both Emma and I are the ones who have appointments today. Luna picks at the food left on her plate. Giving her arm a nudge, I grab her attention. "You don't have to go. You can stay here." I try to ease her mind thinking she may be worried. She shakes her head and straightens her back against the chair.

"No," Raine translates in a stern voice. "I'm tired of being afraid. I'll go," Raine finishes.

I understand how she feels. You reach a point in your life where you have to make a choice, and she's choosing to fight.

With breakfast over, Emma, Luna, and I offer to clean the kitchen since the other women cooked. Almost an hour later, the three of us step outside into the warmth of the mid-morning sun, soaking in the heat of the rays as we wait for Grey to bring the SUV around front.

"Why do you guys call it a cage?" Emma asks Sam.

"You're caged in; you can't feel the sun on your back or the wind in your hair." He tries his best to explain, which seems to satisfy Emma's curiosity.

"Makes sense," she responds. Her eyes follow the truck as it pulls up. Sam opens the door and joins me in the back seat while Luna and Emma buckle in the middle row.

The next few hours go by quickly. The guys even stop by The Cookie Jar for us on our way back through town after leaving New Hope House. This was Luna's first time being in town since getting here a few weeks ago and the first time meeting Jake's wife, Grace. I stare out the window at the green pastures as we pass by several horses grazing behind white fences.

"What are you thinking so hard about over there?" Sam pulls me closer, and I rest my hand on his knee.

"For once—nothing. I usually have a million things running through my head, but right now, I'm free of all of that." I find it strange as I say the words. I don't know how to describe it. Even with threats looming over us, I've felt a sense of calm today. Leaning my head against Sam's shoulder, I listen to the low hum of the truck's engine as we cruise down the highway.

The silence is short lived the moment I look out the window, noticing a small black car driving alongside us in the other lane with an arm hanging out the back window, and in hand is a gun pointed right at our SUV. I shout "Gun!" seconds before the sound of bullets pierce the sides of the truck, and the window shatters, sending shards of glass flying all around us.

"Goddamnit. Go! Go!" Sam roars as he unbuckles. The SUV lurches forward as Grey floors it. Sam turns to me. "Babe, unbuckle, and get the girls on the floor. Get as low as you can. Got it?"

Wasting no time, I do as he says, but before climbing the seat, I kiss him. "I love you." I don't wait to hear him say the words back. Flinging my leg over the back of the seat, I twist my body facing Emma and Luna. The fear in Luna and Emma's eyes causes my stomach to knot. "We need to get down on the floor," I try to keep my voice even and calm and make sure Luna comprehends what I am saying. Understanding, she joins Emma on the floorboard of the SUV between the front and middle seats. There's another couple of loud pops and, suddenly, the SUV pulls hard to the right. Grabbing hold of the bench, I anchor myself to keep from getting flung and look over my shoulder through the windshield just in time to see Grey struggle to gain control of the vehicle as it crosses the middle line into an oncoming semi-truck.

"Shit!" Grey yells, pulling the steering wheel in the opposite direction as hard as he can narrowly avoiding us getting hit.

"What the hell?" Sam snaps.

"Fuck. They shot the tires."

"Shit, man. Floor it. We have three motherfuckers in a car coming at us from behind," Sam yells just as more glass shatters. "Sofia, babe. Listen." I can hear Sam but can't see him. "Is your phone in your pocket, baby?"

I reach into my back pocket and grab my phone. "Yeah." The SUV swerves yet again, the piercing sound of metal scraping together echoes around us when the car chasing us rams into the side of our vehicle.

"I need you to call the guys." Lifting my head, I watch Sam lean out of the broken window with his gun in his hands as he fires off three shots before pulling himself back inside. He looks my way. "Head down, Sofia."

Focusing, I tuck my head down past the edge of the seat and pull up my contacts. Logan's number is the first one I come to, so I swipe the screen and put the phone to my ear. "Talk to me," Logan answers.

"Logan, someone is shooting at us," the urgency in my voice catches his attention.

"Tell me where you're at, sweetheart."

More shots ring out. Hearing a bullet hit the truck causes me to flinch. "Um, we're on the highway. I'm not sure how close we are to the clubhouse. Logan, they shot out our tires."

"Shit." I hear movement and Logan exchanging words with someone. "Listen to me. Keep Luna and Emma calm and do exactly what Sam and Grey tell you. They will keep you safe. We're on our way." My phone is knocked from my hand when the car sideswipes us again, causing it to slide under the seat.

"Sam, I'm not sure how much further we can go. We're about to lose rubber. As soon as we leave the pavement and hit the dirt road leading to the compound, they will dig into the ground, and we won't get much further!" Grey yells.

Luna, Emma, and I continue to huddle close together as we hunker down. Time slows to a crawl. "Hold on!" Grey calls out as the SUV takes a hard-left turn. The paved road turns to dirt, and I hold my breath, knowing we are close to the clubhouse.

17

SAM

A cloud of dust engulfs the SUV as we come to a stop on the dirt road down from the clubhouse. The only sounds I hear is the pounding of my own heart and the soft cries coming from Luna, Emma, and Sofia. Grey and I both keep our heads down not knowing if we've been followed or even surrounded. Sofia was on the phone with one of the guys, so my hope is they're on their way. I take a chance and lift my head enough to see if I can get a look at our surroundings.

"You see anyone?" Grey questions and I shake my head.

"Not a fuckin' thing."

"Shit," he mutters.

Just then, the rumble of several Harleys fills the air. Not knowing if it's Savage Outlaw or Kings, I stay vigilant.

"Get ready," Grey warns, then we both fling open our doors, crouch down on the ground and take aim. I hear the bikes getting closer the same moment the dust cloud around us begins to settle. Through the thick fog, I make out Jake, Logan, and Gabriel's forms as they climb off their bikes and run in our direction. Grey and I both sigh in relief.

"We're okay!" I call out then immediately check on Sofia. Ripping the back door of the SUV open, my girl throws herself into my arms.

"What the hell happened!" Jake bellows as he makes his way over to us. I watch as he takes in Sofia's appearance as well as Luna and Emma, who is being comforted by Grey.

I shake my head. "We were ambushed. Motherfuckers came out of nowhere and started shootin' at us," I explain. "The moment we turned onto the dirt road, they tucked tail and ran."

"Son of a bitch!" he roars. "Alright, men. Sam, Grey, I want you two to take the girls down to the clubhouse." Jake looks to Logan and Gabriel. "Call the brothers. Tell them to get the women and children here now, and you two do the same. I'm going to get Grace then pick Remi up from school. We're on lockdown. Let's move." With the orders made, we all act and do as we're told.

An hour later, the clubhouse is a full-on frenzy. Sofia is held up in Luna's room trying to keep her calm. Emma jumps in to help Raine and Ember with the children while the other women scramble to organize.

"Prospect!" Logan shouts from across the main room of the clubhouse. "I need you to go to the storage room downstairs next to the basement and bring up the cots. Bella and the old ladies want the kids to bunk in the playroom."

"You got it." Just as I'm about to walk off, Jake stops me. "Ember and Raine will help ya. They're going to stay with the kids. We have company rollin' in, and they have agreed to give up their rooms for our guests."

"What guests?" Logan asks, walking up behind Jake, but I don't stick around to find out the answer. When I get to the playroom, I can't help but smile at all the kids. I spot Alba sitting on a beanbag chair reading a book to her son.

"Hey, little momma."

She smiles. "Hey."

Crouching down to eye level, I hold my fist out to little Gabe, and he gives it a bump. "Hey, big man." He smiles back but doesn't say anything. Gabe is sweet like his momma but is a boy of few words like his father.

With a worried look on her face, Alba asks, "How's Sofia, Luna, and Emma doing? Gabriel told me a little about what happened. They must be pretty shaken up."

"Luna is a bit shaken. Sofia is with her now. Emma was rattled but is keeping busy by chippin' in around here. It's probably helping her keep her mind off what happened."

Alba sighs. "I know you can't tell me the details of what's going on, but promise me you'll be careful. You're one of my best friends, Sam."

"I'll be careful, little momma. No worries." Standing, I give her a wink and wave to Gabe. "See ya, dude."

After I'm done setting up the cots in the playroom, Jake sends Quinn and me to the warehouse. This is my first time coming to the warehouse, so I'm not exactly sure what the club keeps stored here. Hopping out of the van, I follow Quinn. I wait as he fishes a key from his pocket and unlocks the padlock. Once the door is open, he flips a few switches illuminating the room—the large warehouse is filled with dozens of crates. Quinn strides over to the left side of the room to where a roll-up door is located. The same door the van is backed up to outside. "Hit that red switch behind ya, man." I punch the switch, and the roll-up door opens. "Let's get this shit loaded and back to the clubhouse," Quinn gestures toward the crates. Using a crowbar, he pops the lid to the first wooden box exposing a massive array of artillery. Without question, I begin to transfer the weapons from the container to the back of the van.

I'm lost in thought while trying to finish the task at hand when Quinn interrupts. "You know I never had any doubt about you, man. When Prez came to the brothers with the idea of you

CRYSTAL DANIELS & SANDY ALVAREZ

becoming a prospect, I was fuckin' stoked about the idea. All bullshit aside, I want you to know, you're makin' the club proud. The way you manned up and claimed your woman and the way you've been puttin' your ass on the line for her and us." Quinn leans back against the stack of crates behind him, kicks his foot up, and lights a cigarette. "You're going to make one hell of a brother."

"I appreciate that, man."

He tosses his cigarette to the floor and stubs it with his boot. "Teatime is over. Let's finish up before we both start growin' pussies." He smirks.

I shake my head and chuckle. Quinn sure as hell is one of a kind.

When we arrive back at the clubhouse, things appear to have settled down. The guys are huddled around the bar drinking while looking to be deep in conversation. Quinn and I saddle up at the bar with them. Just as I'm about to take a swig of the beer Ember passed me, the door to the clubhouse opens. With every man in the room on high alert, we're on our feet in seconds. "I heard some trash has rolled into town, so I came to offer my assistance," Demetri announces as he strides across the room, followed by his right-hand Victor and his son Nikolai.

"Hey, dad," Logan steps to Demetri. They pull each other in for a side hug and clap each other on the back. Logan does the same with his brother. "Thanks for comin' down."

"Alright, Prez," Logan quips. "We got everyone here. Are you going to let us in on the plan?"

"I'm still waitin' on a few more brothers," Jake takes a pull of his beer. The men share puzzled looks as to who Jake is referring to the same time he pulls out his phone, taps the screen, then gives us a full-on grin. "Our guests have arrived." The unmistakable sound of engines rumbling draws everyone's attention and we all file out of the clubhouse to greet our visitors. Pulling up on their bikes is Riggs, Kiwi, and Fender from the Louisiana chapter. Riggs, The Kings Louisiana President, cuts his bike engine and climbs off. "Hope we're not late for the party."

"Just on fuckin' time, brother," Jake offers his hand. Once Riggs' men dismount their bikes, there is a round of handshakes before Jake leads them inside to the bar for a drink. The second we step inside the clubhouse, Lisa, Bella, Alba, and Mila file out of the kitchen to see what the commotion is and trailing behind them are a few of their kids. Cutting my eyes toward the far corner of the room, I see Sofia standing at the edge of the hallway silently surveying the reunion. Seeming a tad uncomfortable with the number of men here, I stride in her direction. "Firefly," I murmur in her ear as I pull her into my arms. "You okay, baby?"

"I'm okay. I was coming to see what all the noise was. I didn't know Riggs and his men were coming into town," Sofia sighs, sounding tired. "I should get back to Luna. She's not holding up too well."

"She still out of sorts with what went down today? I hope she knows she is safe here at the clubhouse."

"It's not that. Luna knows this is the safest place for us." Sofia shakes her head and lays her head on my chest. "She's blaming herself for putting the club and me in danger. I tried explaining to her nobody here is angry at her or blames her for what's happened."

I pull back and take my woman's face in my hands. "You're amazing. You know that?" I kiss her lips. "Luna is lucky to have you in her corner."

"Prospect!" Jake bellows. "Come here. Both of ya." He motions for me and Sofia to join him and his brothers.

"Do you know what's going on?" Sofia asks as I take her hand in mine and lead her across the room to where Jake, Riggs, and the rest of the men are standing.

"Not a clue, babe."

Keeping Sofia close to my side, I step up to Jake and Riggs. Jake makes the introductions. "Riggs, this is Sam, and you remember Sofia."

I stick my hand out. "Nice to meet you, sir."

"You can call me Riggs." We shake hands, and I nod.

Riggs then turns his attention to my girl. "How ya doin', darlin'?"

"Doing okay. It's nice to see you again."

"Sofia," Jake breaks in. "You remember me telling you I had a plan in the works for Luna?" She nods.

"I believe the best way to keep her safe is to get her out of Polson. Riggs has agreed to help."

"What do you mean?"

"I want you to help me convince Luna to go back to Louisiana with Riggs. She will be under his protection. He'll get her settled and keep her safe. This is her best bet at starting over."

Sofia closes her eyes and takes a shuttered breath. "I don't know if she'll agree. Luna is already skittish around you all. I can't imagine how she'll react, knowing we want her to leave with Riggs."

Riggs cuts in. "Bring her out. I want to talk with her," he grunts. Sofia leaves and returns a few minutes later with Luna in tow, and walking alongside them is Raine. I watch the way Riggs becomes laser focused the moment his eyes lock on Luna. She looks terrified—ready to flee at any given moment. Riggs' stare is intense, and Luna has a hard time keeping eye contact. Sofia gives a reassuring nod before she begins to speak. "Jake has come up with a solution for keeping you safe." Raine, who we found out knows sign language, translates Sofia's words to Luna. Luna signs back, and Raine speaks for her. "What's the plan?"

Sofia points toward Riggs. "This is Riggs. He's the President for The Kings Louisiana Chapter. Jake would like for you to go back to

Louisiana with him. The club thinks it would be for the best if you left Polson."

Luna's eyes dart frantically back and forth between Jake and Riggs. Her chest starts heaving like she's on the verge of a panic attack. Sofia turns toward her friend, placing her hands on her shoulders. "Luna. Rex knows where you are. If you continue to stay here, you will not be safe."

Luna closes her eyes, visibly gulping. What happens next shocks the hell out of everyone in the room. Riggs takes two steps forward, going toe to toe with Luna. He places his finger under her chin and tilts her head back. Luna's eyes widen with the sudden contact. Her gaze stays fixed on the large man standing before her. Once satisfied that he has Luna's complete attention, Riggs lifts his hands and begins to sign. "You don't need to be scared of me, Mon Tresor. My men and I will keep you safe. I promise." He speaks out loud so the rest of us understand what he is telling her.

Luna signs, and Raine speaks for her. "I don't want to put any more lives in danger. My mess has caused enough harm. I think it's best I leave on my own." Luna's lip trembles. Sofia was right. Her guilt is eating her up inside. It's to the point she's willing to risk her life to keep everyone here safe.

"No," Riggs cuts her off with a growl. "The decision has been made. You're coming back to New Orleans with me." Luna's look of worry is replaced with one of anger as she narrows her eyes at Riggs

"You can't just decide something like that. You can't boss me around." Her hands move quickly.

Riggs grins. "Looks like I just did, sweetheart." Luna huffs, placing her hands on her hips. She's about to protest once again before Jake decides to end the spat.

"Alright. That's enough."

"Come on now, Prez," Quinn smiles. "Where's the popcorn? This shit was getting interesting. I want to see what happens."

"Jesus fuckin' Christ," Gabriel grunts. The rest of us, myself included, can't help but chuckle. Leave it to Quinn to break up an intense moment, although intense is a bit of an understatement. Right now, the vibes coming off Riggs could set the clubhouse on fire. Without another word, Luna turns and walks out of the room. "I'll talk to her," Sofia says taking off after her. Jake claps Riggs on the back. "Let's get a drink." Over the next couple of hours, Jake lays out our plan of attack against Savage Outlaw. "Alright brothers." Jake stands. "Let's turn in and get some shut eye. Tomorrow we go huntin'."

18

SOFIA

As safe as I feel lying next to Sam, I can't sleep. Every time I close my eyes, I see the end of a gun pointing in our direction all over again. Despite the fact that I kept my calm during the entire ordeal, I feel like I'm barely hanging on. Yesterday I didn't have time to do all that. I was more focused on keeping Luna and Emma calm rather than focus on my feelings.

Reaching over, I grab my phone from the nightstand. Pressing the side button, I check the time. 3:00 am. People will start waking before long, so I decide to go ahead and get out of bed. I slide myself from beneath the covers trying not to disturb Sam. Standing, I look down at him and watch his chest rise and fall with every breath, then my stomach knots up when thoughts of losing him surface. He could have gotten shot yesterday. Taking a deep breath, I push those thoughts aside because that didn't happen. He's here, and focusing on that is more important.

With light footsteps, I cross the bedroom quietly, opening and closing the door behind me as I step into the dim-lit hallway. Thinking about making some warm milk and honey to calm my nerves, I pad down the hall. Luna's cracked bedroom door catches my attention. *Odd.* Not even at New Hope House did she sleep with her door ajar. Pushing the door open, I peek inside and notice her bed made. Stepping in, I look around the room. Something's not right. Leaving, I make my way downstairs hoping I find her in the kitchen, but she isn't there. However, I notice the sliding door partially open. Crossing the kitchen, I notice the alarm has been disarmed as well. I wasn't even aware she knew the code, but it's possible she paid attention when Lisa locked up last night. I slide the door open and step out on the patio. There's a slight early morning chill that causes my skin to break out in bumps. Crossing my arms, I glance around the backyard, straining to see past the yard because of dense fog. Instinctively, I open my mouth to call her name but catch myself. *Crap.* My good sense tells me to go back inside and wake Sam, but my feet carry me forward. Something stronger is telling me Luna is out there.

I step off the concrete patio. The grass beneath my bare feet becomes damp from the dew covering the grass. I stay along the edge of the clubhouse until I reach the corner of the building. I then step out further in the yard to get a better look. That's when I think I see something off in the distance, in the direction of the compound gate. The fog is beginning to lift but still dense enough I can't see the fence line. Moving out a little further, I make my way toward the front of the building stopping by the tree where several vehicles are parked. That's when I catch sight of Luna walking toward the gate with her bag in her right hand. What is she thinking? Avoiding the gravel beneath my bare feet, I stay on the grass and jog in her direction. As soon as I catch up to her, I grab her by the arm, causing her to spin around swinging her bag in my direction as she does so. Unable to avoid it, the bag slams into my shoulder. Her eyes widen when she realizes I'm the one standing there with my fingers gripping her forearm. Her face falls and her eyes well up with unshed tears. I look at her. "What are you doing?"

Her only response is to shake her head before trying to pull free from my hold, but I refuse to let her go. She was trying to leave. I won't let her run.

Before I can tug her back and get her to look my way, I hear a low click just behind my right shoulder.

"Don't fuckin move," a gritty voice murmurs. My heart jumps into my throat. I recognize the voice. It belongs to the man who attacked me—Pike. Luna spins in my direction when my grip on her arm tightens to the point my nails dig into her skin. Her mouth drops open as she looks past me. I feel the cold metal press against my temple, knowing right away I have the barrel of a gun at my head. Standing stone-cold still, I look at Luna and mouth run. Tears stream down her cheeks as she refuses to move. Pike steps to my side, but I keep my eyes on Luna.

He snaps his fingers, and Luna's eyes shift to him instead. "I know you read lips, so pay attention. Keep walking in that direction, or you'll watch her take her last breath." He violently jabs the barrel of his gun against my head. I drop my hand from Luna's arm. Her eyes shift back to me, and I try once more mouthing for her to run. I see it. The look in her eyes the very second she makes her choice. I feel tears threatening to break free because I realize she is giving up. Every fiber of my being wants to scream; wants to fight back but I don't. I can hear myself yelling inside my head, but no words or sound ever leave my lips. I watch as Luna turns her back and begins to walk. With the gun pressed hard against my flesh, I follow.

It's quiet outside. Dead silent as we walk across the property cloaked in the foggy morning mist. Focusing on keeping my anxiety in check, I count the steps I take. When I reach 180 steps, the fence surrounding the property on the backside, near the old barn shed, comes into view. This is only the second time I have been back on this side of the property. I'm not allowed back here but last summer I did a little exploring during a family BBQ and found myself out this way. I stare at the sturdy old wood structure as we walk past. I never did go inside. Something stopped me. My steps slow.

"Fuckin' get to steppin', bitch," Pike shoves me hard enough to make me stumble into Luna's back. She turns, her face soaked from tears, and I cling to her. Grabbing her by the hand, I don't let go. Pike steps in front of us and points his gun in our faces. "I said, keep moving." I take a good look at him—tall, broad. His hair is dark, cut short. His face scarred. Burn scars I think, but only on one side of his face. "Don't fuckin stare at me bitch," he snarls then cracks the palm of his hand across my cheek. It stings, but I suck it up. I've been hit a lot harder than that. Showing defiance, I lift my eyes to his, glaring, showing my hatred for him. He smirks. "The guys are gonna love breakin' you. Let's go." Bile rises in my throat at his threat.

We stop at the fence. On the other side, we watch two more guys appear from behind the tree line, weapons drawn. "You have got to be the luckiest fucker I know. How in the hell did you get her?" one of them says, pointing to Luna.

"Stop with the fuckin question and lift the chain-link you asshole, before we get caught." Pike looks behind us. The fog is thinner than it was, making it much easier to see the outline of the clubhouse in the distance. Pushing us forward, he instructs "Crawl." Luna goes first. The two guys on the other side aim their guns at us. Getting on my stomach, I pull myself under the fence, and I'm yanked to my feet. Luna latches onto my hand. She's trying very hard to keep her eyes on what they are saying.

"Who the fuck is this?" the shorter man, with shaggy red hair questions, and points his gun at me after his buddy clears the fence.

"We'll discuss it as soon as we get our asses away from here." He brushes the dirt off his pant legs. I look at the other two men. They must be bikers too, but they are not wearing cuts.

"This was not part of the plan, man." The redhead grabs me by the arm and shoves me to the ground, causing me to land on my knees. Luna is pulled away by the other guy as the red-headed man hovers above me. "Orders were to place the bomb, wait for it to blow, move in, get the bitch, and leave." He presses the barrel of his pistol between my eyes, and I stop breathing. "This is not part of the fucking plan." The one who took us points his gun at his friend.

"You fuckin question my authority again motherfucker, I'll make you dig your own grave before I kill you and toss you in it." He cocks his gun. "As VP, I'm in charge while my brother sits behind bars." He squares off with the redhead. The man lowers his weapon. "Get the fuck up," he growls at me, and I follow his orders.

Disappearing amongst the trees, we walk for a few minutes before coming out near a narrow dirt road where a rusted blue moving van is parked. The backdoor is already open, and we are instructed to climb inside. Luna and I huddle together with our backs pressed against the wall. The one claiming to be the VP— my attacker, jumps in with the short bald guy and closes the doors, while the other climbs in the driver's seat. There are no seats in the back, just a couple of crates. The only window is a cut out between the bed and the cab of the van, and the only light comes from a small dome above our heads.

The VP narrows his eyes to slits, staring at us for a few minutes as the van starts and we begin to drive down the bumpy road. I realize the moment we hit the highway because the ride becomes smoother. Turning my head, I look at Luna. Her attention is trained on the man sitting across from us. Her tears have stopped, and her face has dried. Pike pulls a cigarette from the front pocket of his shirt. As it dangles from the corner of his mouth, he digs a small square matchbook from the same pocket. Lifting his foot, he strikes a match across the bottom of his boot, brings the flame to the tip of the cigarette and lights it. He cocks his head and blows out a cloud of smoke. "I never understood what my brother saw in you." He takes another drag.

"You should be dead right now. If it were up to me, you would be. However, my brother still has a hard-on for you." He flicks ashes to the van floor. "He's getting out soon. Did you know that?" Pike smirks. I feel Luna's body stiffen. "Rex has plans for you." His eyes shift to mine. Leaning forward, he puts his elbows on his knees, then blows smoke in my face. "And you." He licks his thin, dry lips. "You just happen to be my consolation prize for putting up with my brother's sick obsession with your friend here." His hand reaches out, grasping my knee. His touch causes me to recoil.

"Don't touch me," I find my voice.

"Or what?" He grabs me again, this time forcing his hand between my thighs. Without thinking about the repercussions, I bring my foot up, kicking him in the chest with as much force as I can, sending him stumbling back against the box crate he was sitting on. He recovers quickly and in a matter of seconds, snatches me by the hair on my head, tossing me across the back of the moving van. "Fighting makes me harder." He grabs his crotch as he stands over me. "I'm gonna use you up. Then I'll let the rest of the club have their turn. I'll have you begging me to kill you before it's over." His words drip with venom making me remember Antonio and Los Demonios. Trying to put more space between myself and my captor, I press my back against the corner near the backdoor. I stay put for the remainder of the ride.

I've been listening to the sound of the wiper blades, and heavy rain hit the roof of the vehicle for a short time now. If I had to take a guess, we have been on the road for at least thirty minutes. Pike stands from his seat and maneuvers himself to the front of the van talking in hushed tones to the driver. With his back turned, and the red headed guy's attention turned toward the front as well, Luna crawls across the van floor. "My family will find us. Don't give up. No matter what happens, you fight," I mouth to her. A new look of strength and determination shines in her eyes, and she nods. A sharp turn jostles us from side to side before feeling the van come to a halt. The men turn around catching the two of us huddled together again.

"Home sweet home," Pike announces.

With a loud bang coming from the outside, Luna and I move to the side as the door opens and appearing in front of us are five more men staring back at us, sporting cuts with the name Savage Outlaw. "Out," Pike barks.

Once Luna and I shuffle out of the van, I take in our surroundings. We are inside a vast industrial building. Plastic covers the broken windows. "Take them upstairs. I'll deal with them later. Someone bring me my fuckin' phone. And bring me a damn beer," Pike orders and walks off in the opposite direction of where Luna and I are dragged to.

They lead the two of us past several large pieces of machinery —one of which is a conveyer belt and the other a massive round saw blade. After climbing the rickety metal staircase to the second floor overlooking the warehouse, we are taken into a room that looks to have been a janitor's closet at one point. The smell is the first thing I can't ignore the moment we are shoved inside. A rotten, putrid smell mixed with a strong odor of mold. A man pushes his way inside the cramped space holding a pair of handcuffs. He slips them through the backside of a large pipe protruding from the floor, leading up the wall through the ceiling. The redhead from before grabs my wrist, painfully twisting it as he forces my hand above my head and the other guy slaps one cuff around my wrist. Treating Luna in the same manner, he brings her hand above her head as well next to mine as the man tightens the other cuff around Luna's wrist.

Both men step out of the small room. Neither one bothers looking back before closing the door leaving Luna and me in utter darkness.

19

SAM

It's been fifty-two minutes since Reid woke the entire clubhouse announcing Sofia and Luna were missing. The motion sensors surrounding the property line of the compound were tripped and sent an alert to his phone. By the time I jumped out of bed and raced outside to the back of the compound along the tree line, they were long gone. The tire tracks in the mud were the only evidence left behind by the men who are minutes away from meeting their maker. At that exact moment, something inside me shifted; a switch had been flipped. Something dark and ugly had crawled up inside me and took residence. Something unfamiliar but welcoming. Standing outside, with the rain beating down on my head, my eyes focused on the tire tracks that lead away from the compound. I breathed in the warm, damp air and allowed the bleak darkness of the night to consume my entire being as I made a silent vow to bring Sofia home and end the man who has taken her from me. My fingers twitched at the thought of having them wrapped around the son of a bitch's neck. With those evil thoughts running through my brain, my body vibrated with adrenaline, and my blood began to boil. On the inside, I'm burning up, but on the outside, I'm a mask of calm. The eerie stillness that surrounded me said don't fuck with me because moments ago while standing outside in the haunting silence with the other men, I said nothing as I turned and walked away in the direction of the clubhouse. I was on a mission with only one thing on my mind. I heard Quinn calling out my name seconds before Jake murmured, "Best let him be, brother. He's got that look."

I snap back to the present when a black duffle bag is dropped at my feet. "Suit up," Gabriel says with the same look of determination and fury that mars the face of every man in the room. Forty-five minutes ago, we all watched as Reid showed us the video from when Sofia and Luna were abducted. It all started when Luna snuck out of the clubhouse. A minute later, Sofia came into the picture as she walked out of the same door Luna did moments before. I watched on the video as my woman, wearing nothing but her pajamas hustled after Luna who was making her escape across the compound toward the south end of the property. It only took us two seconds to spot what Sofia and Luna didn't because of the fog. A shadowy figure stood just beyond the trees as the orange glow from the end of his cigarette burned through the darkness. The two women had no idea of the danger that waited for them.

At first, a couple of the men had questioned what Luna was doing. Was she willingly meeting with one of Savage Outlaw's men? But that thought was quickly squashed. We all knew what Luna was doing. She was running. Luna had been so eaten up with guilt. She was doing what she thought would help keep Sofia and the club safe. At that, though, I lift my gaze to Riggs who is sitting three feet from me. He's geared up and is currently assembling what is my best guess a bomb. A bomb left behind by Savage Outlaw. Stupid fuckers didn't even have it rigged the right way. It was a dud. But not anymore. Now they will have their own bomb used against them. It looks like a metal box wrapped in black tape. Riggs is using a pair of pliers to fuse an array of wires. It suddenly dawns on me how Riggs got his name. Cocking his head sideways, he eyes me. "I always bring my own toys to the party, but this one will do." After a pause, he speaks again. "We're going to get our women back, brother. You can fuckin' count on it." I don't miss the fact he said, *'our women.'*

I nod. "Only goddamn outcome there is."

Leaving Riggs to do his thing I go about getting ready. The second we finished watching the security feed, Jake had Demetri, and his right-hand guy Victor, along with Nikolai, hit the streets and canvas the area. They started by following the tire tracks while Reid began tapping into the surrounding area traffic cameras. He's been on the phone with Demetri for the past twenty minutes with a lead. We are now waiting for confirmation and a location.

Unzipping the duffle bag, the first thing I pull out is a gun holster. Shrugging my cut off, I slide the holster on over my shoulders then pull my cut back on. Also, in the bag are two pistols and several clips. I load both weapons before sliding them into the holster. Once finished, I stand and take in how quiet the clubhouse has become. Each man stands ready and waiting. I turn my attention to my left to see the women gathered in the hall at the edge of the main room. Each one visibly shook. Sofia is such an essential part of this family and fiercely loved by every person here. She is the last person on the planet that deserves what happened to her. But my woman is strong. She will overcome this just as she did in the past, and I'll be by her side as she does.

Taking a deep breath, I try to rein in my thoughts; the ones that cause a gut-wrenching knot to form in the pit of my stomach. The thoughts I desperately don't want running through my head. What are those filthy animals doing to my girl? Have they touched her?

"Don't go there, son," Jake's gruff voice cuts in as he comes to stand toe to toe in front of me. "I've been in your shoes. I know what you're thinkin'. Right now, you're thinkin' the worst. That can't be helped. What you need to do is take all that shit swarmin' inside your head and turn it into sheer willpower, not anger. Anger will only get you hurt or killed. Anger clouds your judgment, and you forget about being smart. Sofia needs you, and your club needs you. You get what I'm sayin'?"

I nod. "Yes, sir. I get you." Jake is right. I need to keep a clear head. To do so, I have to get my emotions under control. At this moment, I'm thankful for Jake. Grateful he was paying enough attention and saw my struggle. It's one of the many things that makes Jake one hell of a President. I have not once doubted why these men look up to him, and this is why.

"We have our location!" Reid shouts as he stands from the bar shoving his phone in his cut.

"Where?" Jake barks.

"Cocksuckers are held up at the old lumber mill. They were right under our fuckin' noses when we went out that way a few days ago."

"You have got to be fuckin' kiddin' me," I hiss under my breath as I head out the door behind Jake.

Reid continues as we mount our bikes. "Demetri has eyes on the place. He said we're dealing with thirteen Savage Outlaw. He said they'd stay in place until we arrived."

"Alright, brothers!" Jake bellows. "You heard the man. Demetri confirmed thirteen of those motherfuckers have taken up residence at the lumber mill but be prepared for more. Always expect the unexpected. We're goin' in, and we're goin' in hot. We roll in and take those sons of bitches out. You shoot every one of them dead, no questions asked. We don't stop until every man wearin' a Savage cut is on the ground with a bullet in them. I want to see those walls painted red." Jakes starts his engine, and the rest of us men follow suit. Nine strong, we peel out of the compound and head in the direction of the mill. One of Riggs's guys, Fender, stayed behind along with Blake and Bennett to guard the clubhouse. As we ride down Main Street, the power coming from our engines fills the empty road rattling the windows of the buildings lining the street.

It's early morning and still dark as the town of Polson is asleep and blissfully unaware of the bloodshed that's about to take place in their backyard, unaware of the evil that has taken up residence next door. Ignorance is bliss, they say. Those people are lucky. Myself, along with the men I ride with know the truth. We know all about the monsters that live in the shadows, watching and waiting for the opportunity to strike. What the demons don't understand is The Kings are always ready. When you least expect it, we will come for you. We're going to paint the walls red and take back what's ours—what's mine. "I'm comin' for you, Firefly."

With the lumber mill in sight, Jake doesn't slow down, and he doesn't hesitate. He's doing exactly what he said we were going to do. We're riding in hot. I'm sure by now Savage Outlaw has heard us coming. I have no clue where Demetri, Nikolai, and Victor are, but they are no doubt close by and prepared for battle. The lumber mill is a large metal framed industrial building. It has sat empty for several years now. The parking lot had long ago grown over with grass and weeds, and the roof is missing several sheets of metal while the windows are covered in plastic. The moment our Harleys rumble through the busted gate shots begin to ring out.

In a fury of movements, we follow Jake as he leads us behind an abandoned eighteen-wheeler trailer. Parking my bike, I jump off, draw my pistol, and begin returning fire covering Gabriel as he makes his way across the lot to the far-left corner of the abandoned building. Gabriel's position puts him in direct line of the man currently shooting in our direction. He wastes no time taking him out. Gabriel then gives us the all clear to move forward.

"Split up," Jake calls out, and one by one we take off in separate directions. Sprinting from behind the trailer, I quickly make my way around back. I spot a set of stairs leading up to a door on the second level of the mill. Taking two steps at a time, I reach the door only to find it locked. I take a step back and promptly kick the door open. I go to peek around the busted door when a bullet whizzes by my head. With quick-fire reflexes, I take aim and shoot. Besides the other day when our SUV was ambushed, and when Gabriel and I took down those two men on our way to Charley's, it has been years since I've fired a weapon; the last time being when I was on a hunting trip with my grandfather as a teenager, but my grandfather was an excellent hunter, and he taught me well. My aim is spot-on, hitting the man right between his shoulder blades as he cowardly tried to flee. Keeping my weapon raised, I make my way down the hall toward the body lying on the dirty floor. It's not lost on me I just killed a man; murdered another human being and felt absolutely no remorse. Maybe it's the adrenaline, or perhaps it's the hate making me think the way I do. Perhaps it's because ridding the world of one less Savage Outlaw is protecting future victims. That thought alone will have me sleeping like a baby at night.

Stepping over the body at the base of the stairs, I hear rapid gunfire followed by the sound of bullets ricocheting off metal. I descend one step then two, and that's when I see the large filing room. The room is filled with all sorts of heavy machinery and rusted saws. Scanning the room, I spot Jake crouched down behind a band saw that's almost bigger than he is, and that's also when I see a Savage Outlaw not twenty feet in front of me firing in Jake's direction.

Without hesitation, I raise my weapon, take aim, and fire a single shot to the back of his head. Jake and I acknowledge each other with a brief nod. Side by side the two of us move through the room but stop short when we hear someone screaming for help. I turn to Jake. "You hear that?"

"Yeah, I heard." We're both quiet for a second when we hear the call again. It's muffled, but there's no mistaking who the voice belongs to.

"Sofia!" I yell and take off down the hall leading away from the filing room with Jake hot on my heels. "Sofia!" I shout again, this time the plea sounding closer.

"Sam! I'm here!" A banging noise accompanies Sofia's screams. Stopping in front of a closed door, I try turning the handle only to find it locked.

"Sam!"

"I'm here, baby. Hold on." I notice the door padlocked from the outside. "I need something to break the lock," I say out loud.

"Here." Jake hands me a metal pipe. Gripping the pipe in my hand, I bring it down on the lock, breaking it open. I toss the pipe to the floor and fling the closet door open. We find both women handcuffed to a pipe on the wall.

"Shit," I tug on the cuffs and turn toward Jake. "What can we use to break them free?"

"Let me check that fucker over there." Jake points to his left at the end of the hall where a man lies dead. "If we're lucky, the key will be on him." Turning, he walks away, kneels over the body and rummages through the guy's pockets. It doesn't take long and he's returning with several keys on a metal keyring in his hand. He begins sifting through them. "Bingo." Passing the key to me, I waste no time unlocking Luna and Sofia.

"Oh god, Sam," Sofia sobs, throwing herself into my arms.

"I got you, Firefly." I hold her tight. A feeling of relief passes through me, and I don't know how I'll ever be able to let her go again.

Riggs walks into the room. "Did you find..." his words are cut off when he sees me holding Sofia. He then cuts his eyes over to the closet, where Jake is trying to coax a terrified Luna out. Riggs places his hand on Jake's shoulder. "I got her brother. You two go on. We're all clear. Our brothers are waitin'."

"You get that cocksucker Pike?" Jake asks. With a pissed off grim expression, Riggs shakes his head. The anger radiating off Jake is evident. He nods. "Let's go."

With Sofia still in my arms, I carry her as Jake leads us out of the building to where the men are waiting on us. "Don't look, baby," I tell Sofia, shielding her from the dead bodies and bloodshed littering the ground around us. Stopping beside my bike, I place Sofia on her feet. The sun is beginning to rise, and I'm getting a good look at the damage to her face. I cup her cheeks and place a gentle kiss on her swollen lips. She begins to cry harder as her body trembles. Sliding off my cut, I drape it over her shoulders. "Put this on." I have a thousand questions I want to ask but refrain from doing so. My top priority is getting my woman away from this place and back to where she feels safe. Straddling my bike, I hold out my hand. Sofia takes it and climbs on behind me then wraps her arms tight around my waist as she lays her head against my back. A few seconds later, we watch as Riggs exits the building with Luna's hand in his. They stop at his bike, and he signs something to her. Luna bites her lip and nods. Riggs climbs on his motorcycle before Luna slides on behind him.

"Let's go home," Jake grunts, and we fire up our bikes. One by one we fall into formation behind our Prez as he leads us away from the lumber mill. When we get about a half a mile down the road, Riggs retrieves a small device from his cut and holds it above his head. His thumb presses down firmly on the switch. Without warning a ground-shaking explosion erupts behind us and I watch in my side mirror as the lumber mill erupts into a cloud of dust, broken metal and orange flames light the sky behind us.

Twenty minutes later, we arrive back at the compound. The sound of our bikes alerts the old ladies, and they waste no time filing outside each one wanting to check on their men. When

Emerson emerges from inside her eyes find Quinn first, but when she sees he is unharmed, he gives her a look, and she makes her way to Sofia. The look on Emerson's face says she is in full doctor mode. By the time she reaches us, I've already climbed off my bike and have my girl in my arms. "Sofia?" Emerson speaks in a soft tone.

"I'm okay," my girl says in a shaky voice that means she's anything but okay.

"I'd still like to check you over, sweetheart." Emerson cuts her eyes to me, looking for help.

"Baby," I lift her chin. "Will you go with Emerson so she can check you over and get you changed? Please," I urge, knowing it's what's best. I kiss her. "I won't be far behind, okay," I assure. Sofia agrees and allows Emerson to lead her inside. Once the women have seen their men are no worse for wear, they follow behind Emerson taking Luna with them.

With the women out of earshot, Jake speaks up. "I want you all to go get cleaned up, see to your families, have a few stiff drinks, then I'm callin' church. That cocksucker Pike slipped by us. We need to figure out our next move."

"Has anyone seen Demetri?" Quinn cuts in. We look at each other and shake our heads. Just as Jake is about to open his mouth, Demetri's black SUV rolls through the gates of the compound. "Speak of the devil," Quinn grins.

Victor exits the driver's side the same moment, Demetri and Nikolai step out of the back. "Where the hell did you three disappear too, brother?" Jake asks Demetri, his tone was teasing.

"You know I like to show up bearing gifts," Demetri smiles. Aside from a little bit a blood splatter on his suit, he looks just as put together as usual. Demetri signals to Victor who walks around to the back of the SUV. Opening the hatch, we watch as he pulls a limp body out. Striding toward us with the body draped over his shoulder, Victor stops in front of Jake and drops Pike to the ground. We all look from Pike to Demetri's smug face.

Jake shakes his head and chuckles. "Always showin' up and dumpin' bodies. I got to say, brother, I like your gifts." Jake then turns to Gabriel. "Take him to the basement. The rest of you go have that drink and rest up because later we play."

20

SOFIA

Following Emerson up the stairs, she leads me into mine and Sam's room. My shoulders sag as I lower myself to the bed. I become lost inside my head as my thoughts drift. My brain starts playing my last few hours of events over and over again, like a movie reel. The truth, I'm surprised I haven't lost control of the emotions swirling inside me. That might have something to do with the fact that up until now, I had someone else besides myself to think about. Channeling all my fears into taking care of Luna kept me focused. I had to listen for both of us. The closet we were handcuffed and locked inside was also completely void of light when they closed the door. I could hear every crude comment said about us from the men who were taunting us from the other side of the door.

Then real fear set in when I heard gunfire and men yelling below us. My first thought wasn't of myself. I knew The Kings had come for us. The bullets I listened to as they ricocheted off the metal walls of the building meant they were putting their lives in danger to save us, which meant Sam was down there somewhere amongst the chaos too. *What if he dies?* That thought began repeatedly playing in my head as I kept hold of Luna's hand there in that dark musty closet. When I heard heavy footsteps ascending the stairs, where we were being held, I mentally prepared myself for the worst—to die. Then I heard Sam's voice and relief washed over me.

Sam did his best to shield me from the bloodshed as we made our way out of the lumber mill, but it was hard not to notice the vacant look of death in a few of the dead men's eyes as we walked by.

"Sofia." The bed dips beside me. "Are you okay with me taking a look at you?" Emerson questions her tone gentle. "Besides the visible marks on your face, are there any other places you were hurt?" Ironic now that I'm safe, I can't find my voice. All I can do is stare at the wall. My eyes fixed on a single crack on the painted surface.

"Sofia." Bella steps in my line of sight, breaking the trance. Lifting my eyes, I take in her concerned expression and blink. Glancing to my left, I find Alba, Grace, Mila, and a somber Luna looking back at me. It's weird how you can be very present in a room with other people but somehow feel so far away at the same time. My eyes are drawn back to Bella as she steps closer and kneels on the floor in front of me. "Did any of those men sexually touch you?" she asks the one question I know is weighing on all their hearts considering they know what I have been through in the past.

"No." I keep my answer short, but I do not doubt if my family hadn't shown up when they did my truth would be much different. I make eye contact with Luna, who has taken a seat in the chair next to the bedroom window. There's a light knock on the door before it cracks open, and Raine peeks in.

"May I come in?"

"Sure," Alba tells her. Stepping in, Raine closes the door.

"Ember and Lisa are with the kids. I wanted to make sure Sofia and Luna were doing okay." She looks my way, and I give her a small nod. She turns in Luna's direction and signs. Luna gives her a slight nod as well.

Looking around the room, I take in so many important people in my life. The women in this room are my sisters. That thought alone causes me to break down. It's the love I feel at this moment that has me losing it. Tears streaming down my cheeks drip onto my hands, resting on my lap. And they let me cry. Without question, my sisters gather around me as I sit on the edge of the bed and let it all out. They even cry with me as I let go of the past —all of it.

After having a moment to collect myself, I give Emerson the go-ahead to check me over. By the end of her examination, I am mentally and physically exhausted. All I want to do is take a hot shower, slip into one of Sam's shirts, and crawl into bed. Once the women pass out their hugs, they leave. Thirty minutes later, my tired body slides into bed. Missing Sam's arms, I wrap the blanket tight around my body and bury my face in his pillow inhaling his smell which instantly relaxes me. Before long, my eyes grow heavy and I drift off to sleep.

21

SAM

"Logan said I would find you out here." I whip my head around to find Jake striding in my direction, his boots crunching on the gravel. I checked on Sofia twenty minutes ago and found her passed out in my bed, so I decided to come outside for some fresh air. Looking up at the dark cloud-covered sky, I inhale the warm Montana air.

"Needed a breather," I say as Jake takes a seat in a chair across from me. He's silent for a moment as he takes his cigarettes from the inside of his cut, puts one in his mouth and lights it. He says nothing as he takes a long drag. Neither one of us says a word for several more minutes while he continues taking one pull after another from his cigarette.

"How's Sofia?" he asks.

"She's okay. Finally fell asleep about twenty minutes ago."

"Emerson check her out?"

I tip my chin. "Yeah. Her face is a little banged up, but she's good."

Jake nods, satisfied with my answer. "Some shit went down tonight," Jake points out changing the subject, and I nod in agreement. He continues. "Wanted to see where your head was at on all that."

Leaning forward in the chair, I rest my elbows on my knees and level Jake with a look. "Truthfully, I'm good." I cock my head to the side and look off into the distance as I try to conjure the right words to say, but Jake beats me to it, somehow knowing exactly what was on my mind.

"You have no regrets about what went down and ending those two pieces of shit, but it bothers you that it doesn't bother you. Am I right?"

I sigh and run my hand down my face.

Jake scoots to the edge of his seat, coming face to face with me. "I'm going to tell you the same thing I told each one of my brothers the first time they took a life while protecting this club. Believe it or not, we all have felt the same as you are feeling now. We've faced our own conflicting emotions. The reason you feel no remorse for ending the lives of two men today is that those pussies deserved the bullet they got. Because had you not taken them down, there is no telling how many more innocent lives they would have taken—innocent people like Sofia and Luna. That is not something you'd be able to live with. There will be many people who will not agree with our brand of justice, who don't understand why we choose to go above the law but that's what separates us from the rest of the world. We don't need them to understand nor do we need their approval. The only thing that matters is protecting the club, protecting our family, and keeping our town safe. If that makes us bad people, then so be it. I'm more than ready to answer to my maker for my choices when my time on earth is done. That's the only question you should be askin' yourself right now. Are you prepared to answer for your sins when you're standin' outside those pearly gates?" Jake stands and clutches my shoulder. "The choice is yours, son." With those parting words, he walks off. I watch his retreating form as he disappears inside the clubhouse. I have a feeling Jake's speech was his way of giving me an out.

I also know he would respect my decision to leave if that is what it came down to, but at the end of the day, there is nothing to think about. Am I prepared to kill again if faced with the same circumstances as today? The answer is always yes. Am I ready to answer for my sins when my time on earth is up? Hell, yeah. The club is my home now, and The Kings are my family. There is nothing to decide. Standing, I make my way across the lot and into the clubhouse behind Jake. When I open the door, he's standing just inside the entrance with a crooked smile on his face. "My gut is never wrong. Now let's go take care of the son of a bitch downstairs." I follow Jake the same moment, Logan, Gabriel, Reid, Quinn, Grey, Blake, and Austin stand from the bar and do the same.

On the way to the basement, we pass Demetri and Nikolai in the hall. "We'll be on our way, friend, unless you need us to stay."

Jake shakes his head. "We'll take it from here, brother. Thanks again." Jake claps Demetri on the shoulder, and with a nod, he and Nikolai take their leave. When we come upon the basement door, Jake halts and turns to us. "I want to find out everything there is to know about Pike's brother before we end him. Riggs will be leaving out in a few hours with Luna. The more we know about Rex, the better. Riggs needs to know what he's dealing with to protect Luna better."

Entering the basement, we're met by Riggs, Kiwi, and Fender. Cuffed to a chair with duct tape covering his bloody mouth is Pike. Stalking up to Pike, Jake rips the tape away from his mouth, where he promptly spits a mouth full of blood at Jake's feet. Pike's actions earn him a fist to his ugly mug. When the asshole lifts his face, the curved shape of his nose tells us it's broken. I look down at Jakes' hand to see he has slipped his brass knuckles on. I've heard several of the guys mention in the past brass knuckles are Jake's favorite tool. "You'd be smart to watch your fuckin' mouth," he snarls. "Your compliance won't save you, but it will determine how swift your death will be. Personally, I couldn't care less either way." When Pike makes no move to talk, Jake continues. "Tell me what Rex knows about Luna and who is feeding him the information."

"My brother gets his intel from one of the guards at the jail. I don't fuckin' know which one. Besides," Pike looks up at Jake with a sinister smile as blood drips from his nose and over his mouth, "Rex was released two days ago. It turns out the authorities don't even need that bitch of his. The charges against my brother were dropped due to insufficient evidence."

"Fuck," Riggs hisses, and Pike begins to cackle.

"You assholes are so fucked. My brother will not stop until he gets what he wants, and for whatever reason, he wants that deaf bitch. Don't know why he'd want the whore."

No sooner do the words leave his mouth, Riggs flies across the room. He begins to pummel Pike with one harsh blow after another, sending the chair and him to the concrete floor. After more punches than I can count, Riggs backs away, his chest heaving. A nearly passed out Pike sputters and coughs out two teeth onto the basement floor.

Through shuttered breaths and wheezing, Pike adds, "Rex is coming for her. He won't stop until he gets back what's his."

"He'll never touch Luna again," Riggs says with venom in his tone. "I look forward to the day I send your brother straight to hell, right beside you." With nothing left to say, Riggs stalks out of the basement with his two men Kiwi and Fender, behind him. If I had to guess, I'd say he's on a mission. That mission being Luna.

"Was it something I said?" Pike chuckles. "You know," he continues to run his mouth, "I never did agree with my brother's taste in bitches. Personally, I like them a bit younger with dark hair." He licks his lips and sets his sights on me, where I'm currently propped up against the wall. On the outside, I look relaxed—almost bored, but on the inside, I feel my rage rising because I know I am not going to like what's about to come out of the prick's mouth.

"I like hair so long I can wrap it around my fist while I force my cock into their mouth." I push off the wall and take one step—then two in Pike's direction, never breaking eye contact. "It's a pity I didn't get my chance with Luna's little friend. I would have had a good time fucking every one of her holes. Once I was done with her, I would have let my brothers have a go at her too," he spews.

Stopping in front of the worthless piece of shit, I reach into my cut and pull out my gun. Jake nor do any of the other men make a move to stop me. I know it's because they feel it's my place and my right to take out the man who hurt my woman and dared to take her from me. At this point, Pike knows his fate and chooses to add fuel to the fire burning inside me. The part of me that will do anything to keep my promise to Sofia. To honor the vow I made always to protect her.

"You want to know what I would have done after we finished making her our whore?"

"No," I say, cutting him off from uttering another word the same moment I raise my pistol, firing a single shot. With a single bullet, I kept my promise to my girl, and just as I knew I would, I feel nothing but relief.

Feeling the heavy weight of a hand on my shoulder, I snap out of my daze and turn to see Jake at my side. His look is one of understanding and pride. It's not the act of taking a life that gives him satisfaction; it's my willingness to protect the club and our family by any means necessary. When I glance over my shoulder at the other men in the room, I notice their faces mirror that of their President. I have their approval as well. "Son," Jake draws my attention back to him. "You're done for tonight. Go to your woman."

Without argument, I follow orders. Being the man and the

President, he is, Jake knows that being with Sofia is precisely what I need right now. Leaving the event that just occurred down in the basement behind me, I step into my room and quietly close the door, careful not to wake my girl. Closing my eyes, I take a deep breath and allow some of the tension to leave my body. Looking at Sofia sleeping safely in my bed fills me with peace. Stripping out of my clothes, I climb into bed next to her and pull her body flush against mine, my actions waking her from slumber.

"Sam, is everything okay?" her sleep-filled voice asks with worry.

I hold her tighter. "It is now." I kiss her neck. "Close your eyes, Firefly. I got you." With my whole world in my arms, I close my eyes, breathe Sofia in, and fall asleep with her.

The next morning the whole family stands outside the clubhouse as Riggs, Kiwi, and Fender prepare to hit the road back to Louisiana. Sofia is standing next to Riggs' bike, hugging Luna goodbye. At the end of the day and with the new-found revelation, Rex is a free man. Luna made the safe choice going with Riggs. Although I don't think he would have allowed her to choose otherwise. With Raine's help, Sofia communicates with Luna and promises to stay in touch. The two have become close, and though Sofia hates to see Luna go, she knows it's for the best. Luna's safety is at stake.

With a round of hugs and handshakes, the men mount their bikes. Holding out his hand, Riggs helps Luna climb on behind him. He gives Jake one final salute over his shoulder before he and his men ride through the gate. When the sounds of their Harleys' can no longer be heard, Jake turns to us.

"How about some breakfast?"

"Fuck yeah!" Quinn rubs his stomach. "Feed me, love me, and tell me I'm pretty."

EPILOGUE

Sam

S IX MONTHS LATER

"ARE YOU EXCITED ABOUT TONIGHT?" Sofia asks from her perch on the bathroom counter. I turn the knob in the shower cutting the water off before stepping out of the stall. I don't miss the way her eyes drink in my wet body. Her heated gaze and the way her tongue darts out, licking her bottom lip, causes my cock to stand at attention. Teasing her, I decide to take my time reaching for a towel before wrapping it around my waist. Once I've covered my body, Sofia's eyes finally dart away from my dick and up to my face, where I reward her with a knowing smirk. Leaning in I plant a kiss on her lips. "I fuckin' love your blush." Sofia rolls her eyes. "And to answer your question, I'm stoked. I thought it would be at least a year before I earned my patch." It's true. I was floored when

Jake randomly announced last week I would be patched in and tonight the club will make it official.

"What do you think you'd be doing with your life right now had you not met the club?" Sofia asks.

Stepping between her parted legs from where she sits, I place my hands on her hips. "To tell you the truth, I haven't thought about it. Nothing else is an option. This is where I am meant to be. My life is you and The Kings. I can't imagine anything different. The day I moved to Polson, and the day I first laid eyes on you, my world shifted, and I knew I had found everything I was searching for."

Sofia rests her arms on my shoulder. "I get what you're saying. After I lost my parents and was tossed into the dark depths of hell, I never gave up hope that one day I would make it out and find a place I could start over. The Kings saved me. They may not be blood, but they are my family. Then you came along. You gave me your love, and I gave you my heart. But most importantly, I have found peace."

"You have my heart too. You have all of me, Firefly," I say, pulling her closer and kissing her hard. It doesn't take long before our kiss turns heated. Grabbing hold of her hips, I pull Sofia's ass to the edge of the counter making the shirt she is wearing ride up. I'm pleased to find she is not wearing anything underneath and her glistening pussy is on full display. Sliding her hand between our bodies, she releases the towel around my waist and my hard cock springs free. Having gained more confidence in recent months, Sofia wastes no time taking my dick in her hand and lining the head up at her entrance. She's just as desperate for me as I am for her. Once I feel the tip kiss her entrance, I thrust forward burying myself in her tight heat. "Fuck," I groan as Sofia throws her head back with a cry.

"Oh, god!"

Bracing myself, I place one hand on the mirror behind her

head, and the other clutching her ass cheek. I drill into her with long hard strokes. Looking down between us, I growl when I see her juices covering my cock. Glancing back up at Sofia's face, I notice her looking down at our joined bodies. "You like watching your man fuck your pussy?" Sofia's lust-filled gaze meets mine, and she nods. "Tell me what you want, baby," I demand on a thrust so hard she gasps. Sofia licks her lips. She is still a little shy about telling me what she needs, but she is getting there.

"I want your mouth on me," she says, cupping her breast.

I smile. If my woman wants my mouth on her tits, then that's what she's going to get. Leaning down, I take her rosy nipple into my mouth, lavishing it with my tongue, the sensation causes her pussy to flutter around my cock. Knowing she is close, I gently bite down on her nipple, which I have learned has a direct connection to her center, and she cries out her orgasm as her pussy spasms around my dick triggering my release.

Time slows as we both try to catch our breath. Sofia looks at me with a lazy, satisfied smile. "I think you need another shower. Want to join me?"

"No. I want to walk around the rest of the day smelling like you."

While Sofia takes a shower and gets ready for tonight's party at the clubhouse, I decide to make us a quick breakfast. I'm not much of a cook, but my mom did teach me how to make French toast. Striding down the hall, I notice Emma's door ajar, but the house is quiet. That means she's probably already left for work. I stayed with Sofia last night. She and I usually take turns. Some nights I stay here, and other nights we stay at the clubhouse. We've talked about moving in together but have decided not to rush things. I'm still getting settled into club life while Sofia is about to start school. We are young and have all the time in the world. As long as she's next to me in bed every night, I have no complaints. I'm gathering the ingredients from the refrigerator when there is a knock at the door. Striding to the large living room window, I peer outside to see a silver car parked behind my bike. When I swing the front door open, I am not at all prepared for who greets me on the other side. "What the hell are you doing here?" I snap, not bothering to hide the venom in my tone.

"Son. I want a minute of your time. Please."

"Sam. Who's at the door?" Sofia asks from behind me.

"My dad," I answer, not taking my eyes off the man standing at the door. "You have a lot of fuckin' nerve showin' your face here," I bite out.

Coming to stand beside me, Sofia places her hand on my arm, and I instantly relax.

"I only want to talk. I want the chance to apologize," he says, shocking me. My father has never apologized to me a day in my life. Sofia squeezes my arm. "Maybe you should hear him out," she whispers so only I can hear. Sofia knows my father is a sore subject and the things he's done are unforgivable in my eyes. He went after the club, and he went after my woman. My dad has no place asking me for anything. With my mind made up, I turn back to the man standing in front of me—the man who looks like my father but doesn't. The man I remember had a certain presence about him. The man staring back at me with pleading eyes is not the William McGregor I once knew. This one is a shell of a man. He looks sad, almost defeated.

With that being said, I still don't have it in me to give a shit. I shake my head. "I have nothing to say to you. You need to get off my woman's porch and get the hell out of Polson." Without another word, I shut the door in my father's face.

Sofia wraps her arms around my middle. "Are you okay?"

I kiss the top of her head. "Yeah, baby. I'm good. I'm not going to let him ruin my day. Now, how about that breakfast?" I ask, wanting to change the subject because the truth is, I'm not sure how I feel about what just happened. My whole life all I wanted was for my dad to show some emotions toward me or to tell me he is sorry for all the shitty things he's done. Him showing up here this morning is a little too late in my book. Making my way back into the kitchen, I begin to finish the task of cooking breakfast. Hearing the front door open, I look over my right shoulder and watch as Sofia walks out on the porch and retrieves an envelope lying on the railing. "What ya got, babe?"

Stepping back inside, Sofia closes the door behind her. "It's from your dad. I saw him leave it before walking away. It has your name on it," she hands the envelope to me.

Plucking the paper from her outreached hand, I stare down at it.

"Do you want to open it alone?"

I shake my head and swallow. "No."

Deciding to rip the band-aid off, I tear open the letter.

Sam,

I wrote this letter in the event you refused to see me. I knew my chances were slim, but I had to take a chance. What is there really to say except I am sorry? I'm sorry for not being the father you needed and giving you the life you deserved. I only wish your mother was still alive so I could say the same words to her. I want you to know how much I cared for your mom. She was the love of my life. You might find that hard to believe, but it's true. I also know your mother's death is on my hands. I didn't honor our vows. I don't remember the point in my life when I let her go, and god help me, I would give anything to have her back. A few months ago, I was sitting in my office at home, and I suddenly realized I was no longer happy. I thought back to the last time in my life when I honestly felt joy. Do you know when that was? It was the day you were born. I never told you this, but the day you came into this world was the happiest day of mine and your mother's life. Your mom made me promise not to turn into my father. She made me promise I would follow my dreams and to teach our child to do the same. I failed her. And I failed you. Unlike you, I gave in to the pressure and became what my father, your grandfather wanted me to be. As the years ticked by that's all I knew and soon enough, I did the same thing to you. I had become my father, and I was trying to turn you into me. What had my behavior gotten me? The love of my life was dead, and my son despised me. A son is supposed to look up to his father, but in our case, Sam, it is me who looks up to you. Your mother raised you right. You grew up to be a man who was determined to go out in the world and find his purpose. I only wish I would have been there to see you become that man. I am grateful to the people you now call family and to Jake Delane for showing you how a father is supposed to be to a son. Enclosed with my letter is the one thing in the world besides you that meant the most to your mother. I hope my gift brings you a little closer to your mom and brings you peace. My gift is not only for you but for my love. It's time I show her I am the man she married all those years ago.

Love always.
Dad.

I finish reading the letter out loud and look over at Sofia, who is sitting beside me on the sofa with tears running down her face. "What did he give you?" she sniffles.

Pulling the second piece of paper from the envelope, I unfold it. For a moment, I think my eyes are playing tricks on me. "I can't believe it," I mutter, scanning over the document a second time. "It's the deed to my grandparent's farm. The one my mother grew up on."

"Oh my god, Sam." Sofia looks down at the paper in my hand.

"Your dad gave you the farm?" she chokes out. "The one he said he sold?"

Swallowing past the lump in my throat, I take a deep breath and try to gather my emotions.

"What are you thinking?"

I blow out a breath. "I don't know. I'm trying to process everything."

Sofia rubs my arm. She doesn't push for more. She knows once I get a handle on what I just read, she'll be the first person I talk to. In the meantime, I can't help the smile that takes over my face. "What do you say we plan a trip to Texas? I want to take you to the place that meant the most to me and my mom."

"I'd say when do we start packing," Sofia beams.

Scooping my woman into my arms, I bury my face in the crook of her neck and breathe in her sweet scent.

"I'm so happy for you, Sam. What a great gift."

A FEW HOURS LATER, Sofia and I arrive at the clubhouse. I take in all the cars and bikes parked outside. Everyone is here this evening for my patch in ceremony. Pulling my bike alongside Blake's, I put the kickstand down and shut off the engine. I help my woman with her helmet. She shakes out her hair, then looks at me as she runs her fingers through the scruff growing on my face

"I'm so proud of you," she beams.

Placing my finger beneath her chin, I tilt her head back and capture her lips with mine.

A long drawn out whistle interrupts our heated kiss. "Now that's how you kiss a woman," Quinn teases. Sofia buries her face against my chest. I press my lips on top of her head. "Come on, babe." I grab her by the hand, and we make our way toward the front door where Quinn is leaning against the brick wall.

"You ready?" Quinn pushes off the wall.

"Born ready."

As soon as we walk inside, the room erupts with cheers. "Son, get your ass up here." Jake waves me over to the bar, and the room falls silent. "Everyone knows why we're here—to make our prospect a permanent part of the King family. Sam has proven his loyalty to not only the members of this club but to our families as well. He has shown his dedication to our laws and has shown the willingness to lay down his life for one of our own." Jake glances at my woman who is standing with the other old ladies on the far side of the room, with love in her eyes. I watch Logan stride over with a leather cut in his grasp and hand it over to our President. Jake holds it out before me. I take in the Kings logo and the Montana bottom rocker. "You've earned the right to wear The Kings of Retribution on your back. I know I speak for every man in this room tonight when I say we are damn proud to call you our brother." Jake—my Prez, calling me his brother, gets me choked up. I know what being brother means to these men—now my family —my brotherhood. The room rumbles with *hell yeah* and clapping. Shrugging off my prospect cut, I hand it to Ember who is standing behind the bar. Jake gives me my new cut, and I slip it on. The significance of it sinks in as I feel the weight of it on my shoulders.

Jake grins at me. "Feels good, doesn't it, son?"

I nod.

"The floor is all yours brother." He steps to the side.

I rub the back of my neck. "For a long time, I felt lost. I felt like I was missin' somethin' in my life but could never put my finger on what that something was." Searching for Sofia in the crowd, my eyes connect with hers. "I found everything right here in Polson. I found a place to hang my hat. I found my family. My future." Tears pool in Sofia's eyes, and she smiles at me. "I found my home."

Logan raises his beer in the air, and all my brothers follow suit. "To Sam."

"To Sam!" they all yell.

Sofia weaves her way past Logan, Gabriel, Quinn, Reid, and the other men, throwing herself straight into my arms. "You happy?" Her beautiful eyes shine brightly as she looks at me.

"Only one thing could make me happier."

"And what would that be?"

Scooping Sofia off the floor, I hold her in my arms. "Kiss me." Grabbing my face in the palm of her hands, Sofia gently kisses me, her lips smiling against mine.

"I love you, Sam McGregor."

"I love you more, Firefly."

A WEEK LATER, Sofia is riding shotgun next to me with my hand tucked between her knees as we travel down a dirt road in an old Ford pickup truck my father kept in his garage that once belonged to my grandfather.

"There." I point out the passenger window as the house comes into view. The house is a breathtaking two-story white country home—the kind you only see in movies.

"It's—Sam, this place is impressive."

I take in the wrap around porch, and the tall windows that span all sides of the home. The place hasn't changed much. Off in the distance back behind the house, I take in the fact the smaller house the ranch hands stayed in is still standing.

"Look at the size of the windows," Sofia mentions as the truck rolls to a stop.

"Central air wasn't a thing back when my great grandparents built this home. Those windows were their only means of cooling the inside of the house back then." I put the truck in park and turn the engine off. "Come on."

Opening the truck door, I step out and look at my woman with a boyish grin. "Ready?" Sliding across the bench seat, she places her hand in mine. Gripping her hips once she reaches the edge of the bench seat, I lift her out of the truck, and we walk hand in hand up the porch steps to the front door. Unlocking the door, we step inside.

Everywhere I look, furniture is covered with white sheets. Walking over to the staircase leading to the second floor, I run my finger along the railing. Dirt accumulates on the tip of my finger with the years of dust collected on the surface of the dark wood. Memories of summers spent out here flood my mind.

"Can we see the kitchen? My mom always told me when I was a little girl, the heart of the home is the kitchen." Sofia roams what was once the family room lifting sheets to peek beneath them.

I lead the way through an open door into the kitchen. I pause a moment to take it all in. In the center of the large room is the biggest dining table known to man. To my left is a stone hearth big enough a child could stand upright in.

"Look at the size of this thing?" Sofia walks the length of the table.

"My great grandmother had my great grandfather build it because she liked to feed everyone at the same time—the family and the ranch hands," I explain as she runs her hand across the large chair at the head of the table. "That was my grandad's seat and his father's before him." I smile, remembering my grandad's deep, gravelly voice. "No one picked up a fork to eat until the man sitting in this chair said a blessing over the food prepared for us."

I recount other childhood memories as we continue our tour through the home. The entire time I'm also thinking about the many new memories I want to create with Sofia by my side. We step out onto the second story veranda that overlooks the green pastures the cattle once roamed. Sofia places her hands on top of the railing. The setting sun casts a warm glow over her face as she takes it all in. "Sam, this place is beautiful. You are so blessed to have grown up in such a wonderful place."

Walking behind her, I drape my arms around her. "I can picture our kids running around the yard already," I freely admit.

"Kids, huh?"

"When the time is right, yeah, babe, I want kids. We could bring them to the farm a couple of times a year. I'll teach them all the things my grandfather taught me." Sofia spins in my arms and faces me. "But, I got to marry ya first."

"Yeah?"

"Yeah, Firefly. Someday soon, I'm gonna make you mine forever." Resting my hand on her hip, I pull her closer. Her breasts flatten against my chest, and her hands find their way beneath my shirt.

"Mrs. McGregor has a nice ring to it." Sofia's eyes sparkle.

"You're damn right it does."